GRAVE
IMAGES

GRAVE IMAGES

SCHOLASTIC INC.

ISBN 978-0-545-65338-1

Copyright © 2013 by Jenny Goebel. All rights reserved. Published by Scholastic Inc. SCHOLASTIC and associated logos are trademarks and/or registered trademarks of Scholastic Inc.

12 11 10 9 8 7 6 5 4 3 2 1   14 15 16 17 18 19/0

Printed in the U.S.A.   40

First Scholastic paperback printing, January 2014

The text is set in Adobe Caslon.
Book design by Christopher Stengel

For Matt:

You make my heart feel full.

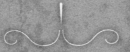

Gold is for the mistress — silver for the maid —
Copper for the craftsman cunning at his trade.
"Good!" said the Baron, sitting in his hall,
"But Iron — Cold Iron — is master of them all."

- RUDYARD KIPLING -

CHAPTER
ONE

THE REASON I NEVER ACT SAINTLY IS 'CAUSE I'VE GOT TOO much want in my heart. Mama was cursed with a wanting heart, too. That's why hers is broken now.

You see, want always seems to drag a heartache right along with it. It's also something that can get you darn near dead when it's the wrong thing you're wanting after.

Trust me, I know.

I also know, when it's right, want can get you the whole blue-green world. The trick is figuring out which is which. And I had a lot of figuring out to do when it came to Abbot Stein.

When he walked into our family work place, I pegged Mr. Stein as one of those poor souls Dad calls "struck by lightning." I saw him as an earnest, devastated, sorrow-dripping-out-of-his-pockets griever. And grievers are the worst part of being in a business that revolves around dead people.

But, to be honest, if the trade is something that calls to you, like it did my grandpa, owning a monument company isn't such a bad way to go. No creepy stiff bodies. No bug-eyed faces to stitch shut. No trying to make a three-day-old corpse look like a living, breathing person simply taking an afternoon nap. It's just about dealing with people full of sadness and making headstones as hard and cold as death itself.

Then again, the headstones themselves are really kind of beautiful if you try to forget what they're used for. Slabs of granite with flecks of quartz and monuments made of swirly marble. Smooth crevices you can dip fingers in and trace the letters of a name and a person's entire history between two dates.

The morning Mr. Stein barged into our lives, Dad was setting to work on one beauty of a marker, tall and sleek with a natural, unpolished edge. Dad didn't know it, but I had my own ideas for what should be carved into the massive piece of rock. I thought if I could take over a bit of his load around Alpine Monuments — I mean doing the real stuff, like coming up with marker designs, not just the housekeeping and errands — he'd have more time to spend with Mama. And Mama certainly needed more attention than any block of stone, no matter how large and beautiful it was.

I'd worked hard on my sketch. I'd done everything I could to make my design good enough for the headstone. But the thing is: Antlers are tricky. I hadn't wanted the buck to look top-heavy, so instead, I might've drawn his antlers too small. It most likely wasn't good enough, yet I was getting up the nerve to show it to Dad anyway when Mr. Stein opened the glass door to our den.

Almost thankful for the distraction, I dropped my sketch of the deer behind Mimi's desk and let it roll back up on itself.

I peered through the open archway connecting the den (which doubled as a showroom) to the garage. Dad was already raising his head. His sandblasting stencils were strewn across the concrete floor, and the sizeable headstone rose at a sharp angle between us. Crumbles of stone dusted everything.

Dad shifted his gaze toward me before lifting his eye protection, and then we both took in the appearance of the distraught-looking stranger. The man's choppy salt-and-pepper hair stood on end like it'd been blown wayward by the wind, except it was a perfectly calm and sunny July day. He wore a heavy black overcoat buttoned all wrong in the ridiculous heat, and his long face was so sunken in, his eyes so hungry, I'd have bet he hadn't eaten for days.

I might've grabbed his hand and led him to a chair to wait until Mimi came around (my grandmother's great with the ones whose feet have been pulled out from under them), except when I started toward Mr. Stein, I got a funny feeling. There was something off about him — something that caused the blood in my heart to race straight down to my legs, making them feel all heavy and stuck to the floor.

Out of the corner of my eye, I could see my father removing his face mask. "Can I help you?" he called out. He didn't usually deal with the customers (or me, for that matter), and his deep voice did nothing to hide how put-out he felt. When the answer he was looking for never came, Dad finally shed his work gloves. He entered the den with a frown and heavy footsteps.

I picked up a rag and faked like I had been too absorbed with dusting a row of display urns to be hospitable to the stranger.

Handling people going through such a hard time took patience, a smidgen of restraint, and a whole lot of tenderness. Dad never could manage the right balance of it all, nor did I imagine he wanted to. He preferred the flat, polished stones to sobbing, heartbroken souls. Can't say I blamed him. But Mimi was off delivering banana-nut muffins to a funeral reception at Sacred Heart, and here I was pretending to be quite concerned with the gleam of each and every urn.

I was sorry for making Dad drop what he was doing, but at the same time, I felt relieved. I'd sat in with my grandmother recently as she was comforting a family and presenting them with various epitaph ideas. To say the least, it hadn't gone well.

At one point, the elderly aunt turned to me and said, "Why, young lady, you've been silent this whole time." It was true; I'd been keeping my mouth shut, and for good reason. But then she pressed further. "Why don't you tell us what you'd want people to say if you were the one who'd died?"

Mimi nodded at me encouragingly, and so I thought about it and then gave my very best, most honest answer. I said, "Well, ma'am, I think I'd want them to say, 'Look, she's still moving.'" Problem was, I felt sincere about my answer, but the aunt thought I meant to be disrespectful, and the whole thing just went downhill from there.

So I thought it best for all if I hung back on this one

anyway. I did, however, turn and stand in a position where I could keep dusting and still watch what was going on. The stranger unbuttoned his overcoat and pulled out a thin, jagged piece of black granite from an inside pocket. He then handed the granite to my father without ever saying a word. As soon as my father's fingers wrapped around the tile, his expression changed. He no longer appeared put-out. He looked like he couldn't quite believe what he was seeing.

The catch of my father's breath followed by his low, soft whistle was enough to make me drop the dust rag and go on over for a look-see.

My own breath stuck just shy of my lips as I inspected the portrait engraved on the stone.

The detail was amazing — far beyond what could ever be achieved with our old sandblaster — and we were well aware of the type of machinery an etching like this required. We just couldn't afford it. However, what made the portrait special was not the fact that we couldn't have made it ourselves. It was the woman's face that drew us in like horses to a salt lick.

She was hauntingly beautiful.

Her round, clever eyes seemed oddly alive — even frozen like they were in the cold, hard granite — and she was far too young for a gravestone portrait. I felt a slight twinge of sorrow just knowing she was dead.

I wished I could tell the color of her hair, but etchings were always a ghostly gray. Pale blond or otherwise, the lady looked a lot like Mama with an ocean tide of wavy locks flowing down her back. Of course, that was before Mama got so sad she went and snipped her hair short and lifeless around her ears. Dad must've been thinking about Mama, too, 'cause he seemed unable to pull two words together.

"That's a real nice etching, sir." I spoke up, knowing what my dad would say if he wasn't tongue-tied. "But we've got no use for a fancy laser here. You might want to travel on down the road to one of the touristy towns. They have loads of money to spend on their dead."

Mr. Stein turned toward me. I noticed for the first time that his eyes were wide set and the color of cement. His jaw hardened, the clenched bones obvious on his gaunt face. And, if I wasn't mistaken, I think I heard his teeth grinding together.

I took a step back and lightly bumped my head on Dad's cotton-shirted shoulder. He was a whole foot taller than me, not to mention twice as wide. But the soft thump I gave him was enough to wake Dad from his trance, 'cause right away he said, "My daughter's right."

I turned my head and lifted my chin.

Dad caught me smiling at him, and I hoped like mad he would smile back, but he didn't. "We can't afford a laser, and even if we could, the people around here can't afford the etchings. So we'll keep on sandblasting our headstones, like we always have." As he said this, my dad once again gazed wistfully at the etching of the attractive woman, and then he stepped forward to usher Mr. Stein out the door. "Thanks for stopping by."

Mr. Stein held his ground. "I'm not selling lasers."

My father scratched his head with two fingers and scrunched his great brow, like Mr. Stein was a puzzle he couldn't quite figure out.

"Whatcha doing here, sir, if you're not selling anything?" I felt a surge of sympathy, thinking maybe the man was a griever after all.

"I'm not selling lasers. I etched this portrait myself, with a chisel and a hammer."

Dad pulled the stone from Mr. Stein's hands. He seemed even more dumbfounded as he reexamined the woman's face. "Not too many people still do hand etchings. Kind of a lost art, isn't it?"

I gaped again at the portrait and then at the stranger. Now that I knew he was an artist, and an incredible one at that, I was seeing him in a whole new light. I figured I'd only imagined the wrongness I'd noticed about him before.

Mr. Stein watched my father, his gray eyes never wavering in my direction, but he didn't answer.

"Well, she sure is breathtaking," my father said after a short while, and I wasn't sure if he meant the lady herself or her portrait. "But artwork like this? Now I'm certain we can't afford your services. Thanks again for stopping in. You have a nice day." My heart sank a little when Dad handed the portrait back to Mr. Stein. As it traveled in front of my face, I tried to memorize it, thinking maybe I could re-create it later in my sketch pad. My hopes weren't real high. Like antlers, faces were tricky, too.

Mr. Stein nodded his head, and then turned to leave. He was almost to the door when he stopped, and said in a voice barely above a whisper, "I've fallen on some hard times. What I'm most in need of is a roof over my head and food in my stomach."

"Hmmmm." Dad rubbed his hand over the gray and brown hairs sprouting from his chin. I knew he was thinking about the old carriage house behind the garage. Even though he came off like a grizzly sometimes, deep down Dad was the biggest sucker of us all when it came to hard-luck cases. More than a few headstones in the Stratwood Cemetery were placed there on nothing more than empty pocketbooks and the kindness in my father's heart. Plus, good, cheap labor was hard to find, and Dad had been desperate for some since Grandpa died. My own help may have come cheap, but I was still working on the *good* part.

"We do have the space . . ." Dad said. "If you're willing to work for room and board, plus maybe a small commission, well then, you can stay with us until you get back on your feet."

I sucked in my breath. I hadn't been sure if I wanted the man to stay or not, but as soon as Dad extended the invitation, I started looking at Mr. Stein as one big, giant opportunity. I'd never seen Dad's eyes light up for any of my artwork. And even though Mr. Stein seemed to be shaking slightly with his back still turned to us — like a kite twitching in the wind, slight enough to be carried off on the next big gust — I hoped he'd stick around long enough to teach me a thing or two about etching.

"Of course, I'll have to speak it over with Bernie's grand-mother," Dad added. "She's out at the moment, but when she returns, I know Mimi will be happy to fix you something to eat, and that'll also give her a chance to consider taking in a . . ." Dad paused like he wasn't sure what to call the man. ". . . well, a guest. In the meantime, there's running water and electricity in the carriage house. Why don't you go ahead and settle yourself out there for now?"

Mr. Stein turned back to face us, and it looked as though he had to force his lips to curl into a smile. "Thank you. That would be wonderful."

I finally released my breath and Dad reached out to shake the man's hand. "Fine. Fine. It's settled, then. I'm sure when the people from town see what you can do, they'll be lining up for your etchings. Bernie, please show Mister . . . Mister . . . I don't believe I caught your name."

"Mr. Stein. Abbot Stein."

"Very good. Show Mr. Abbot Stein to the carriage house, would you?" Dad said as he walked back through the archway.

Mr. Stein raised his eyebrows up in two pointy arches. "Shall we?"

"Don't you want to grab your stuff or something first?" I asked.

"Everything I own is right here," Mr. Stein said, unfold-ing his arms like all decent, normal people carry everything they own in their pockets. The overcoat was still unbuttoned, and as he extended his hands, the lapels fell back to reveal an old iron chisel and hammer stuffed inside. They were rusty-looking, but otherwise kinda dull. Not exactly what I'd expected, having seen how sharp and clear the marks on the stone were. Still, there was something creepy about the hammer and chisel, and I couldn't stop myself from shying away from them.

Mr. Stein seemed to notice my reaction, and he quickly threaded the buttons back through the holes on his overcoat. He matched them up correctly this time so that the inside pockets and the tools were once again concealed.

It was silly, not to mention childish, to be frightened by a rusty pair of iron tools, and I straightened up tall as I could. All five feet of me turned on my heels as I said, "Let's go." Then, to prove to myself I hadn't been alarmed by Mr. Stein, nor by what he was carrying in his pockets, I retrieved the sketch I'd tossed behind Mimi's desk.

It seemed horribly bad in comparison to the lovely portrait, but I was gonna show it to him nonetheless. Not to Dad. Not now, at least. But maybe after I'd seen Mr. Stein to the carriage house, he could give me a few pointers. I really did have a lot to learn before I'd be able to take on any of the monument-designing myself, and I felt foolish for thinking otherwise earlier.

Dad had his stencils back in hand, and the sandblasting machine turned on. He didn't even look up as we exited the door behind him. I led Mr. Stein away from all that dust and humming, and we walked down the flagstone path — the path that paved the way to the carriage house.

"Where you from, anyway?" I asked as I kept my back to him and stepped from one salmon-colored paver to the next, avoiding the grassy spots growing in between.

"Silverton," Mr. Stein said.

"Did you carve stones for a living there, too?" Silverton was only about an hour away, and I'd been there a few times myself. Though I didn't recall seeing another monument company when passing through.

"Bernie seems like an odd name for a girl," Mr. Stein said flatly, ignoring my question.

I stopped. With my toes butting up to the edge of a paver, I turned my head and jutted my chin up to face him. "It's short for Bernadette," I said curtly. "I was named after a saint, but since I never act like one, everybody calls me Bernie." Then I clamped my mouth shut and started walking again. Even if his comment was kinda rude, I should've remembered to be nicer. Things weren't exactly bright and cheery around here to begin with, and I didn't need to be unfriendly as well — especially if I still wanted him to take a look at my sketch.

Our land stretches farther than most backyards — though not by much — and all of our blank headstones line the path on either side. It feels an awful lot like having a cemetery right out our back window, even though there aren't any dead people buried there — just a rooster (Mimi's), two guinea pigs (mine), and a dog (Dad's). But, although it's not a *real* cemetery, it is enough to keep most kids my age away — not exactly the most uplifting spot for a hangout. And then, of course, there was my sad, dreary mother, always sobbing at the unexpected.

I stole a glance back at Mr. Stein and tried to gauge whether or not he found the headstones unsettling, but I couldn't tell. I wouldn't have been surprised if he had changed his mind about staying with us. It got a little uncomfortable around here, even for me, with all the teary-eyed grievers stopping by to make their selections.

Michael Romano didn't seem to mind, but he also didn't count. I didn't want *him* hanging around. He had spooked me just a few days prior by jumping out from behind a towering gray monument while I was taking inventory. Since I didn't put it past him to try it again, I braced myself as Mr. Stein and I approached the big blank marker. When no one popped out at us, I relaxed my shoulders.

I didn't want Mr. Stein thinking I was the jumpy sort, so I turned my head and gave him a sugary smile. But his eyes weren't on me; they were taking in the sight of the carriage house.

In any other backyard, it might be considered a coveted playhouse or fort. In ours, the carriage house just adds to the overall freakiness of the Morrison homestead. Never mind the whispery aspen trees and wild columbines growing about. With its triangle-shaped tin roof and weathered planks, the carriage house looks more like a horror movie shack sitting behind all our headstones than a cozy hideout. Not to mention, it only has one window, and it is 'round the back side of the building.

Its unwelcoming sight didn't seem to bother Mr. Stein any, however, as he was smiling a thin smile. I wouldn't say he looked *happy* exactly — though it was difficult to tell, considering his face was naturally as tart as Mimi's rhubarb pie — but he did seem pleased.

I stepped off the stone-paver path and opened up the front door. I sighed as I looked around inside. There was the window with a cream-colored valance, a narrow bed covered with a faded tulip-printed comforter, a small worktable, a sink, and, in the corner, a toilet with an off-white curtain pulled around it.

Everything was rather dusty, and it smelled like swamp — even more than usual due to the combination of heat and humidity we'd had lately. The smell brought back memories of when I'd come out here during Mama's crying spells. Lying on the tulip comforter. Closing my eyes to shut it all out. It had been a while since I'd been in the carriage house. Not because Mama was crying any less, though. I suppose it was 'cause I was getting too old to hide.

I walked over to the worktable and ran my finger across it, parting a sea of dust. By then, Mr. Stein had snuck up behind me and was standing so close, I could hear that weird noise coming from his mouth, like he was grinding his teeth again.

"You can store your tools in the drawer here, if you like," I said as I turned to face him.

"I'd rather keep them with me."

"Okay, then. Welcome home," I said.

He nodded and I noticed his jawbones were indeed horribly tight.

"Uh, one more thing, if you don't mind . . ." I took a deep breath, thinking how my sketch of the deer really *was* embarrassingly bad. Still, I'd rather be wasting this stranger's time with it than my father's. "I'd like to show you my drawing," I blurted out as I quickly unrolled my sketch before Mr. Stein could say anything. I laid it flat on the worktable and smoothed out the curled up edges as best I could.

"It's a buck. See the antlers?" I said. "I thought Dad could make a stencil of it and sandblast it on Mr. Thompson's headstone. You know, the one he's working on . . . Mr. Thompson was a hunter. But maybe you could help me make it better first, or give me a few drawing lessons or something." Really, I was hoping he'd show me how to do some hand-etching, too, but I didn't want to push my luck that far . . . yet.

"I don't draw."

"Oh, so you go straight to the chiseling? Then . . . can I see the woman's portrait again?"

"Maybe some other time," Mr. Stein said, and raised an arm toward the door. I guess his pleasure with the carriage house did not include me in it. Disappointed, but not wanting to ruin my chances of seeing the portrait later, I snatched my sketch off the table. I didn't even bother rolling it before I backed myself through the open entryway and out into the yard.

"Let me know if you need anything," I said, and as I did, Mr. Stein shut the door in my face.

Huh? I wasn't used to adults acting so rudely. Michael Romano, sure, but then again, thirteen-year-old boys aren't exactly known for their manners. Adults are supposed to behave better.

Maybe Mr. Stein just needed some time to settle in, or maybe he really was a creep. Either way, I'm not one to give up easily. When I had my sketch rolled up and more or less shoved into my back pocket, I crept behind the carriage house to the far side with the only window and climbed atop a forgotten granite tile box.

The box was made of cardboard. It was rumpled and broken apart at the edges from all the snowy winters and hot, drying summers it'd sat there. But the stone inside could weather any storm, and it therefore made a strong and stable foot stand.

I slowly rose up on the box — quite thankful Mr. Stein didn't have his eyes aimed at the window. He happened to be sitting on the bed with his back turned to me, looking awfully out of place in the dainty room. This backside view of Mr. Stein, with his unkempt salt-and-pepper hair, reminded me of a wire brush Dad used for cleaning up paint.

Mr. Stein sat still and stiff as a corpse looking at something in his hands. I kept watching, waiting for him to move, but after a while my calf muscle got a cramp in it from all that standing. I finally had to reach down to rub it. I gave it a good kneading, and when I lifted back up, Mr. Stein was on his feet again and standing beside the worktable. I ducked my head and watched as he jiggled out the old drawer that always catches. Then he slipped something black inside it before ramming the drawer shut. I couldn't be sure, but I thought it might've been the granite piece with the woman's portrait. Humph! I was gonna need a much better look than that.

Mr. Stein returned to the bed. He lay down and closed his eyes — just like I'd done a million times. He still wore his heavy black overcoat, and I didn't know how he could stand the heat. However, it didn't appear he was going anywhere anytime soon.

I hopped down from my perch, more determined than ever to make Mr. Stein's arrival work to my advantage. Now that he'd moved into the carriage house with all his artistic talent, it wouldn't matter whether or not he wanted to share his secrets with me. One way or another, I was gonna figure out how he did those etchings. Then, even if he split (and I was betting he would), things would be okay because *I'd* know how to make the portraits. And me knowing how to do more things meant Dad and Mimi could focus on Mama for once instead of all the other grievers in town.

I'd been trying to help Mama myself, but all I seemed capable of doing was reminding her why she was so sad.

I thought everything would at least get a little better after Mr. Stein arrived. Regretfully, I truly did.

CHAPTER TWO

MIMI ALWAYS SAYS YOU CAN'T TRUST AN OLD PERSON WITH A smooth face any more than you can trust a skinny chef. She's proud of every wrinkle earned by way of smile or tear. If what she says is true, the creases on her face are a road map of a life well spent.

As Mimi leaned over our kitchen table and her eyes narrowed in folds behind her wire-rimmed glasses, I described Mr. Stein's portrait of the dead woman as best I could. I left out the part about how the woman looked like Mama. Mimi knew how much I kept pining for Mama to come out of her room. She'd think that was the only reason I'd said it, and not because it was the truth.

When I'd finished, Mimi turned her attention outside the window. The kitchen sat directly below my bedroom and across from the carriage house. Mimi had placed a flower box on the window ledge (probably trying to pretty up the view), but beyond the purple and pink pansies, you could still see most of the headstones and the entire path leading up to what was now Mr. Stein's front door.

My grandmother breathed in deeply through her long, narrow nose. I could tell she didn't like the fact that Dad had opened the carriage house up to a stranger, but was struggling with feeling so. "Well, I suppose feeding him is the right thing to do . . ." she said as she glanced up at the crucifix hanging above the kitchen table.

Due to Mimi loving God first and roosters second, our home holds a scattering of crosses, paintings of the Holy Family, and images of red comb-headed chickens.

As quickly as she'd looked up, Mimi dropped her gaze from the cross and turned it back outside the window. Then she picked up a ceramic bowl — one with hand-painted roosters around the rim, no less — and started giving the hard-boiled eggs inside a good thrashing. I almost mentioned the irony, but decided it wasn't the time.

"Well. We don't have to feed him in this kitchen. You can carry his trays — three times a day, just like your mother's. That way our family mealtimes won't be disturbed by him being at our table."

Our family mealtimes hadn't been the same since Mama started taking her meals in bed. And Dad rarely sat down to eat anyway. Not much to disturb, really. But — just like with the could've-been-roosters Mimi was whipping around to make egg salad — I didn't mention it.

Instead, I said, "Sure, Mimi," thinking that delivering meals out to the carriage house would increase my chances of seeing Mr. Stein etch one of his portraits. It couldn't be that much different from sketching. Both were about taking what you saw in one place and transferring it to another.

I liked the way sketching felt — calming, and like you had control over what you were putting down on paper, even if you were powerless when it came to everything else. I hoped etching would feel the same.

I smiled at the thought and, in turn, Mimi nodded at me and then went back to work smashing and spreading the egg salad between two slices of sourdough bread. Her hair was long and pulled back loosely in a braid. Silvery strands mixed with light blond hair fell in soft wisps around the frames of her glasses. As she stretched on her tiptoes to grab a napkin from a high cupboard, my grandmother reminded me of an aging ballerina.

We really don't resemble each other much at all. Not only do I have dark hair (which will leave me looking like a skunk someday when the white starts to sprout through), I take after Mama in that I'm short, and I got my thickness from Dad. Nobody would ever mistake me for a dancer.

Having retrieved the napkin, Mimi set it and the egg salad sandwich on a plastic tray along with an apple, a dill pickle, and a glass of whole milk. "There. Now bring this out to our guest. I'll have another one ready when you return."

I carried the tray slowly at first, careful not to slosh milk over the sides of the glass — the way I always carried my mama's tray. But next thing I knew, I was thinking about seeing the lady's portrait again, and I was taking big, sloppy, careless steps in a hurry to get back to the carriage house. By the time I reached it, a third of the milk was splattered across the tray, the sandwich bread was soggy, and I probably should've been a tad bit sorry for it. But I wasn't.

I set the tray down on a flagstone paver and whacked my knuckles sharply on the door.

Mr. Stein opened the door with one hand, chisel and hammer in the other. His face was lax this time, but his eyes seemed oddly out of focus. That was until he slid the tools back inside his overcoat. Then his jaw clenched up again and his eyes began darting quickly around the yard behind me.

I glanced over my shoulder, too. No one was there — only a yard full of headstones like always. "Umm . . . It's just me, Bernie. I brought you some lunch," I said, and pointed to his tray.

Mr. Stein's focus finally rested on me, and judging by the way his grip tightened on the door handle, I'd say he was ready to slam the door in my face yet again. However, his hunger must've gotten the better of him. He bent down to pick the tray up off the ground. As he did, I snuck a peek past his bristly head of hair at the worktable behind him. A fresh granite tile lay resting on top.

"Oh," I said. "Orders coming in already?" I inched forward, but the tray and Mr. Stein were blocking my way. "Can I see what you're doing?" I asked, still trying to get a good look over the top of his head.

Mr. Stein straightened up. With the tray in his hands, he took a step back, and this time used his foot to swing the door shut in my face.

Mama's room was dark due to the heavy wool curtains blocking out all the sunlight. When the fuzzy, multicolored spots in my vision finally gave way to bedroom furniture and gray shadows, I shuffled my feet across the carpet and set Mama's tray gently on her nightstand. As I turned to leave, Mama crooned, "Bernie?" Her voice was as soft as a budding leaf and I stopped to listen — not sure if she was truly awake or just talking in her sleep.

Most days, my feelings for Mama were tender. But sometimes, when I grew impatient, they turned bitter and downright unkind. Those days landed me in a great, big pile of shame, and I was glad this day wasn't one of them. I leaned in, waiting to see if Mama would say more.

She did. "Bernie, who were you speaking to? Back by the cottage? I heard a man's voice." Mama spoke no louder than she had before. I looked at the heavy curtains now billowing from a steady breeze. Had Mama been standing by the open window? Not likely. She must've been able to hear us from her bed.

"Dad hired this man, Abbot Stein, to do etchings for the headstones, and I'm gonna learn to do them, too, and then —" I cut myself short when I saw the pained look on Mama's face. I knew she'd rather I be out making friends than devoting all my time to Alpine Monuments, and here I was about to confess my plans to a take over the portrait making so Dad could spend more time with her. That would make her feel even worse — she'd think she was to blame — and Mama didn't need anything else to fret about.

I backed myself up and out of the story altogether. "His portraits are amazing, Mama. He does them with a hammer and a chisel." I could barely see her reaction in the sparse bit of light managing to fight its way through the curtains, but it seemed to soften. As my eyes adjusted further to the darkness, I took a better look. Mama's face was thinner than the lady's in the portrait; longer, too. But there was something in the high cheekbones, the pointed chin, and the wilted way she hung her head that reminded me so much of the woman in Mr. Stein's etching.

"Oh? I'm sure your father is pleased. I'd like to see them sometime . . ." Mama said.

"You should come with me. I'll take you down myself," I offered, words spilling out of my mouth twice as quickly as my mother's.

My mama gave me a smile so small, it almost wasn't there. "Perhaps tomorrow, Bernie. I'm tired now."

I nodded. "Okay, Mama," I said, knowing full well Mama wasn't coming with me to see any etchings. Not the next day, probably not ever.

I left quiet as I came, shuffling my feet right back out of the poorly lit room. Sometimes I thought maybe I could be the one to drag Mama out of the dark place she was stuck in. Then it wouldn't matter how busy Dad and Mimi were. But I was never able to say or do the right thing. Worse, I usually said the wrong thing, and even just the sight of me seemed to pinch Mama's heart more than she could bear. But it wasn't *my* fault that my brother, Thomas, was also born with dark hair and thin lips. It wasn't my fault that Mama couldn't have any more babies and that looking at me always reminded her of what she never had, and of all that she'd lost.

Some of those angry feelings started to boil in the pit of my stomach. I squished them out by thinking of the woman's portrait again and how I'd sketch it later in my pad. If anything could make me feel better, that could. I picked up speed as I raced down the stairs. I still had a boatload of chores to do and was hoping to fit another peek in the carriage house window before Mimi started looking for me to deliver supper trays.

CHAPTER THREE

As it turned out, my spying would have to wait. Three whole days. Three maddeningly frustrating days — for that's how long the storm lasted. Spindly fingers of lightning tore through the sky. Rain fell in hard sheets instead of drops, and Mimi said she hadn't seen the angels in heaven spill so many tears over the earth since she was a little girl. Within minutes our backyard had turned into a tangle of mud puddles and headstones, and the neighbor's jittery dog was barking at his imaginary adversary — THUNDER. All the while, my desire to figure out how Mr. Stein etched that lady's portrait was growing deeper and stronger. However, I thought the storm did one good thing: Its timely arrival more or less forced Mimi into letting Mr. Stein take up residence in the carriage house.

After I had left Mama's room, and after I'd swept off the porch and collected the mail from the box out front, my chores had led me back to the den. There I'd found Mimi shaking her head. She was saying, "Jonathan, we have enough weighing on this household without taking in a drifter. What do we even know about him? I just don't think he can stay."

In response, my father had stared silently out the back window. It was then that the first boom of thunder had rattled the house and the rain had begun its rat-a-tat-tatting on the rooftop. I watched as a ghost of a smile crept onto Dad's face. But by the time he'd swiveled his head toward Mimi, it had faded away. "What would you have me do, then? Turn him out in this weather?"

Of course, she wouldn't. Dad had known that before he'd asked. So Mr. Stein stayed, and the storm and I teamed together to bring him a whole bunch of sopping-wet meals. I was able to balance Mimi's umbrella in the crook of one arm and keep myself dry when I carried his trays, but Mr. Stein's food? Not so much. Not that I tried very hard, either.

The first night of the storm, I set the tray down by my rain-splattered flip-flops and beat the door with my fist, thinking he'd have to let me in for sure with this weather. When Mr. Stein didn't answer, I beat it again — harder and louder, leaving no doubt in my mind that my pounding was heavier than the downpour.

I couldn't imagine he'd gone anywhere. And I hadn't been that pushy about my sketch and seeing the portrait — had I? Maybe he was still sleeping or else he didn't feel like having soggy meat loaf. It's not like I could run around to the window to check. Mimi's umbrella hanging over my head would hardly go unnoticed if he was awake, what with its brightly colored roosters and all.

Yet, Mr. Stein's tray was empty (except for the small ocean pooling in the middle) when I picked it up the next morning and placed a new one by his door. I knocked again. But, for a

second time, he didn't open up. Annoyed and more than a little bit angry, I left his French toast behind, floating like a
sponge in maple syrup and rainwater. How was I ever gonna
learn anything if he refused to even face me?

Right along with the storm, waves of want and longing
were rippling through my heart. It reminded me of the time
my wanting heart had told me to swipe Missy Princeton's pencil. Missy had played at my house once (on one of Mama's
good days). And I thought we both had fun as I chased her,
swirly-whirly, through the headstones. Looking back, maybe it
was just me who was amused. 'Cause from then on she wouldn't
even look my direction, let alone come back to play.

But on the third day of second grade, when Ms. Tennyson
called Missy up, roused the class in a chorus of "Happy
Birthday" and handed over a sparkly sky-blue pencil, I stared
hard at Missy. I knew right then, I would not be spending an
entire school year with nothing but boring yellow number-
two pencils. Wait an entire school year, until the very last day
when Ms. Tennyson celebrated all the summer birthdays?
Not me.

Later, when I stood behind Ms. Tennyson's desk, the sky-
blue pencil sparkling in my red-hot hands, I told Ms. Tennyson
I just couldn't help myself. And it was the truth. The sight of
that pencil had started a flame in my stomach that couldn't be
extinguished until it was mine.

That night, as punishment, Mimi made me copy the Tenth
Commandment one hundred times. *Thou shalt not covet. Thou*

shalt not covet. Thou shalt not covet . . . When I'd finished, I asked Mimi why she didn't make me copy the commandment that says you shouldn't steal. Then I shut up real quick, thinking maybe she'd make me write it a hundred times, too. But she didn't. She just said, "Bernie, you're not a thief. *Covet* is the same as *want*. And *want* is what got you into this mess."

For all of Mimi's hope and my hard laboring, copying down the Tenth Commandment all those years ago hadn't done a lick of good. My wanting or coveting (take your pick) seemed only to have worsened since then. And, like the backyard being drenched by the storm, my heart was flooding with it. This time, my sights weren't on a silly, little blue pencil. They were set on seeing the woman's portrait again.

I tried over and over to get the woman's image copied from my memory onto a page in my sketch pad. It wasn't exactly like using a hammer and chisel, but I thought the practice had to be good for me anyway. I even tried looking at my drawing of Mama, thinking that since the two of them looked so similar, it might help. But it didn't.

I couldn't get anything about the sketch right. I pressed too hard with the lead. Then I erased like mad until I tore a hole in the paper. I couldn't get any depth to show in her eyes. And the shallow groove above her upper lip, that was giving me a heck of a time, too. If I couldn't even re-create the portrait on paper, how would I ever succeed on stone?

I was smudging the lines of a coil of hair with my finger when, around 3:00 PM, the gray-and-black clouds finally cleared like mourners from a funeral. My room brightened, and I stood from my sketch and went to the window. As I was peering down, the carriage house door swung open and an overcoat-clad Mr. Stein stole away into the soggy backyard. He shrank back from the peek-a-boo sunlight and then quickly slinked through the puddles, around the garage, and out of sight.

Seeing my chance, I raced from my room, down the steps, and out the front door just in time to see him turning the corner down the block. Then, smiling at my good fortune, I turned to head back through the showroom entrance and out to the carriage house. I wasn't gonna let Mr. Stein's unwilling behavior keep me from the portrait a minute longer.

I was used to having wants, but the force of this one was beyond anything I could understand. Way beyond normal. Even for me. Sure, I wanted to study the portrait closely — check out the depth of the markings and such. And I *really* wanted to learn a skill that would make me more useful to my family. But there was also something about the way the portrait seemed to be pulling me to it — something odd and perhaps a little frightening . . . If I hadn't been wasting my time trying to figure out *why* I was feeling so anxious, maybe I would've noticed Mr. Finley before I nearly knocked him clear out of the den.

"Oh dear, I'm sorry," Mr. Finley said, trying to recover from the blow I'd dealt him with my shoulder. Mr. Finley was one of those people who felt the need to apologize even when he was the one being trampled. He delivered our mail — always with a whistle and a smile. I thought he must've been delivering a package, otherwise he'd have put the mail in the box out front, but then I recognized the redness of his nose and the drippy, watery eyes — and in mid-July, we were nowhere near cold and flu season.

"Awww, Mr. Finley," I said. "What happened?"

Mr. Finley lost it then — as so many grievers do — having held it together until the very moment he needed his composure to answer a simple question. He dropped to a chair next to Mimi's desk and pulled out a handkerchief. Then he started sobbing so uncontrollably I didn't quite know what to do. "Wait right here," I said. "I'll go get Mimi."

He lifted his head from the red-and-white hankie and grabbed me by the wrist. "I just want something small. Something to remember her by."

"Okay," I said. "Honest, Mr. Finley. I'll be right back."

But Mr. Finley didn't let go. "Maybe something with a picture, so when I visit her grave, I can remember my pretty wife's smiling face," he said.

"All right, Mr. Finley," I said. Then the need to let out a mighty, honking blow must've taken over him, for next thing I knew, I was free, and Mr. Finley had his nose wrapped up in the hankie again.

I made a dash for the kitchen but never made it. As soon as I reached the entrance to the corridor, Dad was calling me back. I turned around. To my surprise, Dad's large frame was there kneeling right beside Mr. Finley and speaking softly — so quietly, I couldn't quite make out what he was saying.

First Mr. Stein, and now this? Dad was dealing with people more these days than I'd ever seen him. What was he gonna do next, start delivering muffins with Mimi? I'd much rather he just hurry up the stairs to see Mama.

"Bernie, I want you to take Mr. Finley home. Help him find a photograph of his wife, and then bring it back here. And, if you can, see if you can get Mr. Finley to rest for a spell. He could use some time to get through this."

I glanced behind me toward the kitchen where Mimi likely hadn't heard a word, and then out the window toward the emptier-than-empty carriage house, and finally at Mr. Finley with his sad, sorrowful eyes. I remembered all the times those eyes had looked twinkly instead of tearful, and I walked back over.

Even though my heart still yanked me toward the carriage house, and even though I was concerned with what might've been left on Mr. Finley's hand after he'd been holding the hankie, I wrapped my fingers around his. "C'mon, Mr. Finley. Stand up," I said. "I'll get you home." I knew it's what Mimi would've done, and if I was trying to help out more, it was the type of thing I had to do, too.

My peek at the portrait would wait.

I led Mr. Finley out the front door and took a look around. "Did you walk here, Mr. Finley?" I asked.

Mr. Finley sniffled and nodded his head.

"Okay, then. We'll just have to walk you back. Whereabouts do you live, anyway?"

"Benton Street."

Benton Street was all the way across Stratwood. "*Well*, we better get started."

I hurried Mr. Finley along as much as you can hurry anyone whose tether has just been cut from the world. I think he might've floated off altogether like a lost balloon if I hadn't been holding on to his arm.

Then, as if I needed anything else to add to this ordeal, halfway to Benton Street, we ran into Michael Romano. He was coming up the sidewalk on a pogo stick. *A pogo stick!* It was thin and silver and Michael was wearing a bright-red helmet. He looked ridiculous, of course — like a giant cherry lollipop springing into the sky. I hadn't seen him since the day he leaped out from behind the gray monument, and I was none too happy to see him again.

"Hiya, Bernie!" he said as the stick hit the ground and he was catapulted back into the air. I had to softly nudge Mr. Finley aside so that we wouldn't both be clobbered.

"Watch where you're going!" I scolded.

Michael continued boinging right by like nothing had happened. Normally, I'd chase him down, or at least toss a handful of pebbles in his path and see how well he could bounce on those, but I had Mr. Finley to tend to. I glanced over, and Mr. Finley had a frightfully dazed look on his face.

He was living through a nightmare already, and I was sure Michael and his pogo stick hadn't helped the matter any. "C'mon," I said, gently tugging on his arm.

When we finally arrived at Mr. Finley's home, I helped him carry a stack of rubber-banded shoe boxes down from the attic. An old grandfather clock tick-tocked the minutes away as we sat in silence in his front room while he looked through the photographs. My legs were well and stuck to the plastic sheet covering the couch, and I'd counted thirty-four liver spots on Mr. Finley's skin by the time he dropped the hankie for good. No more sobbing. Riffling through the boxes of old photographs seemed to have brought back some of his composure.

"When did it happen?" I asked, curious but hoping not to send him over the edge again.

Mourners aren't exactly predictable. Sometimes they pop into Alpine Monuments the very day their loved one passes. Sometimes it takes months. Time doesn't make much difference. Either way, picking out a memorial seems to rub most of them raw.

Mr. Finley looked up at me like he was so lost in his memories, he'd forgotten I was there. "Three days ago. In the evening," he said steadily enough. I nodded and then calculated in my head. That was when the storm had begun, the day Mr. Stein had arrived at Stratwood.

"My missus loved the rain," Mr. Finley continued. "I thought she'd fallen asleep listening to it, but she never moved out of her chair." Mr. Finley looked through the shutters at an empty rocker on the front porch. He looked at it like he could still see his wife sitting in it. I shuddered. Maybe he could.

"I'm real sorry, Mr. Finley," I said.

"Here, this is the one." He handed me a photo of a chipper-looking woman with short, curly gray hair.

"This is a nice pic," I told him. "She looks real happy."

"Doesn't she, now? Always did."

And that's what did it.

Not me asking questions, but the thought of his lovely wife and how happy she was sent Mr. Finley into another fit of weeping. Not sure what else to do, I patted him on the shoulder and quickly left with the picture tucked safely in my back pocket.

I stopped once I was outside on the screened-in front porch. I ran my hand across the smooth wooden arm of the rocking chair and peered back inside. Mr. Finley was crumpled. No longer on a mission to find the perfect photograph, the memories the boxes held seemed to be adding to the heaviness of his heart. There wasn't any more I could do for him, except hope a monument would bring him some small comfort.

As I walked down the cement steps, a car door opened across the street and Mrs. Evans stepped out. She carried a care basket from Sacred Heart Parish. I didn't have to see inside the wicker basket to know what was there: a small arrangement of cut flowers, a spiral-cut ham, a loaf of corn bread, and a jar of fresh honey. But Mrs. Evans brought more care with her than just what was in the basket.

She saw me coming down the steps and she waved. I looked away, pretending not to have noticed, and walked quickly in the opposite direction. Seeing her here like this, about to go inside and do for Mr. Finley what I couldn't, brought back too much of my own pain.

I'd held Mr. Finley's hand, and I'd led him by the arm, but Mrs. Evans would let him pour out his tears and suffering on her shoulder, and then she'd fill him back up inside with soft smiles and warm hugs. Next, she'd suddenly remember a funny story about a time Mrs. Finley did something clever or cute, and she'd help Mr. Finley find a way to laugh through his tears. She did it for all the parishioners who'd lost someone close to them. I'd seen it in my own home too recently to stick around and watch it play out all over again.

CHAPTER
FOUR

IT WAS SUPPER TIME WHEN I GOT BACK. THE SHADOWS WERE long on the ground and distorted from the falling sun. Somehow the day had turned into as big a muddle as our rain-soaked backyard.

With Mrs. Finley's photo in my back pocket, I set a dinner tray down in front of the carriage house. I expected Mr. Stein to ignore my knocking at first, and I wasn't wrong. But I also knew the storm was over, and I could stand there banging away all night if necessary. Finally the door did swing open, and it happened so quickly, it caught me off guard. I didn't have a chance to say anything before Mr. Stein was bending over in front of me and grabbing his tray off the paver.

I couldn't hurdle him. Never was much of a high jumper, or I might've tried. Instead, when he stood up, I put my hand on the door, thinking I could prevent him from shutting it in my face. He saw my hand. He saw me. But he starting pushing the door closed with his foot, nonetheless.

"Now wait a minute," I said. "I have a photo for you."

Mr. Stein's cement-colored eyes weren't dart-y today. They glanced down at his dinner and then pointed straight at me.

"Put it on the tray," he said. His face wasn't angry or even teasing. If anything, he just looked bored.

"Can I at least see the portrait?" Now that I'd finally gotten his attention, I had to give it another shot.

Mr. Stein's eyes widened. Somehow the question seemed to surprise him more than I thought it should. "What portrait, Bernie?" he said slowly, concentrating on my face.

"The woman's, of course. The one you showed Dad and me the day you came here."

Mr. Stein's eyes shrank back to their regular, old, squinty size. He seemed — I don't know — disappointed or something. "No," he said. Then a gleam entered his expression as he bared his teeth and somehow half smiled, half sneered at me. He turned and walked with the tray in his hands, leaving the door wide open behind him.

He'd done it on purpose. Not letting me in when I'd wanted, and now daring me to follow. Which I did, of course. I stepped inside the carriage house, my heart quickening thanks either to the nearness of the portrait or Mr. Stein's odd behavior.

Mr. Stein set the tray on the worktable and then turned back to face me. The shadows, heavier with each passing moment, seemed to claw at me from the corners of the room. With one hand Mr. Stein opened his overcoat, and my eyes again caught sight of the iron tools peeking out of his inside pocket.

"These are much more interesting than her portrait, don't

you think?" Mr. Stein said. "Without them the granite would still just be a piece of rock."

My voice caught in my throat as he pointed to the hammer and chisel like a peddler hawking his goods. The tools were discolored in a way I hadn't noticed before, with dappled patterns of blue and black and purple. Again, I knew there was no reason for them to frighten me so, but I was petrified. Frozen in place.

"Did you know that during the Middle Ages, iron tools were cooked and roasted in bone dust to harden their edges? What went into the darkness of the smithy was a mystery, and more than one blacksmith was burned alive as a witch or wizard." A smile lifted and twisted on Mr. Stein's face. "These tools are . . . special, Bernie. They're very well preserved for their age, don't you think?"

His lower jaw jutted back and forth. His teeth grinded. What I thought had been a nervous tic before, he now used to emphasize his point. He stopped only to say, "Ground bones, Bernie. That's what they used," and then he made more of that god-awful grating noise.

Finally, I thought I understood what was happening. He remembered how the tools had frightened me the first time I'd spied them, and now he was using them to toy with me. He was trying to scare me off so I'd leave him alone about the woman's portrait. No way, but I did feel slightly flattered. I thought this meant he saw me as competition and was worried I'd put him out of a job if I learned to etch properly.

"Here's the photo," I said, fixing my voice to sound disinterested and not in the slightest bit afraid. I held the picture out to Mr. Stein with Mrs. Finley's face smiling back at me. "Just a small portrait will do."

Mr. Stein grinned and then snatched it from my hands. "Thank you, Bernie, for delivering this fine meal, and Mrs. Finley's photograph."

It wasn't until I was back outside, with the setting sun, that I realized I'd held the picture turned away from him the entire time. Now I was scared. Something wasn't right about all this. Instead of going to the kitchen to pick up Mama's tray, I headed to the garage. It took an entire minute of me waving my arms and shouting like a madwoman before Dad finally noticed and took the earplugs out of his ears. "DID YOU TELL MR. STEIN ABOUT THE JOB THAT CAME IN?" I screamed over the sandblasting machine.

"WHAT?" Dad screamed back.

"MRS. FINLEY? DID YOU TELL MR. STEIN ABOUT HER PORTRAIT YET?"

Dad shook his head no, and right away shoved the earplugs back in.

How could that be? If Dad hadn't said anything, how had Mr. Stein known the photo was of Mrs. Finley before he'd even had a chance to look at it? How had he known about Mrs. Finley at all?

I remembered the weird feeling I had the moment Mr. Stein walked through the door of Alpine Monuments — the feeling that there was something off about him. I'd been ignoring it since. Wanting to see the portrait and learn about hand-etchings had somehow pushed it aside, but it was back, and powerfully so.

"Dad," I said. "There's something not right about Mr. Stein . . ." But since he had the entire world shut out, and me with it, I might as well have been talking to myself.

I had a downright horrid dream that night. A large black smelting pot sat in the corner of a darkened room with liquid fire spurting from its lips. A rod of iron glowed as it was lifted from the flame and then pounded flat between a cold iron hammer and an anvil. Beneath the clatter of metal clashing, I thought I heard the sound of bones being scraped and ground into a fine white powder. Or perhaps it was merely a lingering memory of Mr. Stein's teeth grinding. Either way, I awoke startled, cursing our guest for putting that image in my head.

I sat up in bed. In the dim light, the walls of my room looked gray rather than the sea-foam green they were actually painted. Carefully, but with trembling fingers, I took a rolled-up piece of paper from the drawer in my nightstand and spread it flat over my lap. It was a sketch of Mama. Well, actually of Mama *and me*. I hadn't drawn it myself, but I liked it the most, and it was the reason I'd started sketching in the first place. And I was glad I had. There is something about art that gives you hope, and when you try it yourself, sweet relief.

Mama looked so happy in the sketch, and I needed the

reminder that she was capable of it. That someday she might show that sort of heartiness again. As I looked over the sketch, my racing heart slowed. It calmed me, took me away from the bad dream, and carried me back to one of my most favorite days, a day about six months before Thomas was born.

Mama and Dad and I drove to the county fair, me squashed between the two of them on the bench seat of Dad's truck. All the while, my parents kept stealing starry-eyed looks over the top of my head, thinking I didn't see them.

We ate cotton candy at the fair until our fingers were sticky and gooey with globs of pink sugar. Channeling his high-school-baseball-playing days, Dad knocked down some glass bottles and won a stuffed giraffe for me and an elephant for Mama. Then Dad insisted that Mama and I have pencil portraits made. He wanted us to sit together and to be drawn by an artist that did true-to-life sketches. No cheesy cartoon stuff.

I was feeling a little green about the gills having eaten entirely way too much cotton candy, and it showed in the sketch. But my mama . . . You could almost see the joy radiating from her heart . . . and I could almost pretend it was me that put it there and not the spark of life growing in her stomach.

I knew if I took out my own sketch pad and rubbed a little lead on the rough paper, I'd feel even less shaken. It would soothe me. The rhythm of it. Long, smooth lines, followed by shorter, scratchier ones. I could lose myself in a drawing the way Dad did with his sandblasting, but I didn't have the time for it. Even if I was creeped out by Mr. Stein and my bad dream, I couldn't ignore the breakfast trays. I couldn't ignore Mama.

I rolled the paper up and returned it to the drawer. By the time I made it downstairs, Mimi had the trays ready as well as an extra-long list of chores waiting for me. I started right in; best to be busy and keep my mind off things.

After I dropped off the trays (Mama's to her room and Mr. Stein's to the usual paver), I began sweeping. It wasn't long before Mrs. Evans walked through the showroom door. I glanced up from what I was doing. She had the most joyfully plump and round face, framed by ribbons of long black hair. Normally seeing her would perk me up, no matter what kind of crummy day I was having. Yet this time I felt a sudden pang of guilt for not having been friendlier when I'd seen her outside Mr. Finley's house. I should've at least said hello.

My grandmother never minded if I abandoned my duties when Mrs. Evans came by. She'd just serve up a kettle of honey-sweetened breakfast tea and slices of zucchini bread (or whatever she had on hand). There'd be small talk and gossip, mostly about Sacred Heart parishioners. Then Mrs. Evans would head upstairs to visit with Mama, and Mimi and I would return to our chores.

But since I was feeling slightly ashamed and was afraid she might ask me about our brief non-encounter, I just smiled as warmly as I could, and switched to filing paperwork as Mrs. Evans headed off to the kitchen. No sooner had I filed my first invoice than I heard my dad shout, "MOTHER GOOSE! THAT WAS FAST!"

"Mother Goose" was as close to a swear word as we got in the Morrison household. Mimi was dead set against taking the Lord's name in vain (and anything else she deemed vulgar). So when Dad blurted out anything nursery-rhyme related, I knew something big was happening.

I popped my head up from the filing cabinet, and there was Mr. Stein holding out a new portrait for my father to see. This time, I was there and looking right at the portrait with them before Dad could add, "Old Mother Hubbard!"

Mrs. Finley never looked better.

Somehow Mr. Stein had carried her perkiness right out of the photograph and onto the stone. Each curl of her hair was etched in detail, and her cheeks pushed up beneath the bottom corners of her eyes, adding frames to her toothy smile. I'm not gonna lie, I was blown away by Mr. Stein's artistic skills, but looking at the portrait, I felt a prickle of something just beneath my skin. And it wasn't jealousy. Okay, maybe it was, a little. But this new portrait wasn't doing anything to squelch my growing suspicions.

"Mr. Finley will be *very* pleased. How did you manage to get it done so quickly?" Dad asked.

I was wondering the exact same thing — that, and why I was suddenly feeling so cold, other than that I was suspicious and, yeah, a little jealous, too. I felt an aching chill enter my bones like the kind you get when you stay out sledding too long. Was it sadness and downheartedness, brought on by the sight of Mrs. Finley's portrait, that made my blood run cold? Perhaps. But being around death and loss was nothing new to me . . . Whatever it was, no one else seemed to be feeling it.

Mr. Stein gave a frosty smile. "Let's just say I was inspired," he told my father.

"Well, I have to tell you, your timing couldn't be better," Dad said. "I just got this stone here for Mr. Thompson finished, and as soon as I get it placed, I can start setting Mrs. Finley's portrait in a monument for their family."

Dad looked as though Mr. Stein had truly taken some of the weight off his shoulders. He looked downright relieved. I forced myself to take a deep breath thinking that, for his sake, I should try to reel back some of the unease I was feeling. It didn't matter whether I liked Mr. Stein or not, as long as he was making things easier on Dad, right? Maybe it was better that Dad hadn't heard me when I said there was something not right about this man.

At least it was better until I knew for sure . . . I shook off whatever dark cloud was hovering around me, and that's when genius kicked in. It doesn't happen often, but sometimes I'm quite amazed by my own cunning. "Why doesn't Mr. Stein go *with* you to place this stone?" I whacked my knuckles on the hard granite and tried to forget all about Mrs. Finley's portrait. Still playing innocent, I added, "You're always saying you have trouble managing the stones alone since Grandpa died."

"You know, Bernie, you're right. I could use some help,"

Dad said. "What do you say, Abbot? Would you mind giving me a hand?" He seemed almost chipper about the whole thing.

Mr. Stein, however, glared at me as he spoke to my father out of the corner of his mouth. "That's a fine idea. I'd be happy to assist you."

As soon as he and Dad had the marker rigged up and I could hear the noisy engine on Dad's old truck fading in the distance, I sprang into action. I was even more anxious to get inside the carriage house. Not only did I still want to get a good look at the mystery woman's portrait, I also wanted to snoop around a little. I wanted to see if I could find a real reason to be concerned about our guest.

I jiggled the handle of the door to the carriage house first. It was locked, of course. Lucky for me, I knew how to pop open the window latch. I slipped around back, and then once I was standing on top of the granite tile box again, I shifted the weathered window frame from side to side until at last I heard a clink. I slid open the window just far enough to hoist myself through.

As I catapulted up and off the box, I noticed it seemed thinner than the last time I stood there. But I really didn't give it much thought. I was too busy congratulating myself for getting inside. And I was more than a little bit nervous. What if Dad and Mr. Stein forgot something and decided to come back?

I landed on the carriage house floor with a thump and then noted right away that nothing really seemed out of place.

At least Mr. Stein wasn't a sloppy neighbor. The tulip comforter was pulled up neatly on the bed. There was a new toothbrush resting near the sink. And it even appeared as though Mr. Stein had done some dusting. The only eyesore in the entire room was his breakfast tray, stacked with empty dishes by the door, waiting to be put outside and then collected by yours truly.

I began scrutinizing every square inch of the carriage house. I started by lifting up the comforter to look under the bed. There was nothing there other than a broom with firm bristles and a dustpan coated with fine, sharp shards of stone. There were toiletries under the sink (he must've been out to the store, and it occurred to me that might've been where he was headed when I saw him leave after the clouds cleared) and remnants of breakfast in the wastebasket. All in all, everything was even tidier than before. Even the swamp smell was gone.

Still, I was saving the best for last. I went to the worktable and yanked it open.

Stone eyes stared back at me, but hardly the ones I'd been expecting. The eyes in this etching were smaller and half hidden behind a bottle-thick pair of glasses. Well, what now? It wasn't exactly evidence of any wrongdoing, but the etching wasn't of the beautiful lady, either — not even close. This portrait was of an old man, and somewhere or somehow I knew I'd seen his face before.

CHAPTER
FIVE

So what if Mr. Stein had a new stone portrait in his drawer? And did it really matter if the person's face seemed familiar? That's what Mr. Stein did — etch portraits of people. Just because the sight of it made my skin crawl, that didn't mean anything. Maybe I was just jumpier than I thought.

And if Mr. Stein could complete those amazing portraits in less than a day, well, then, good for him. Good for us, too. Seemed like it should take longer, judging by the amount of detail and how long it took Dad to sandblast a marker, not to mention the unfinished pencil sketch I'd started days prior. But maybe it all just added up to the fact that he was really good at what he did. Dad sure seemed to think so.

By the time Dad and Mr. Stein returned from the cemetery, I'd nearly convinced myself that the man's portrait was nothing to worry about. I was back in the den, safe and pretending I'd been there filing paperwork all along. Dad still looked chipper and Mr. Stein's jaw was lax and unmoving. A sign, I thought, that he was feeling as content as he ever got.

No sooner had they walked in the door than Dad scribbled some wording on a piece of paper, handed it to me, and sent me off with a new ad for the church bulletin. All it took after that was a short jog down the block and around the corner, and I could see the metal cross that sat atop Sacred Heart Parish. Beyond it, the mountains looked fuzzy and gray; smog had moved in and blurred their normally sharp edges.

The church sits smack-dab in the heart of Stratwood. Stratwood isn't a real small town. Just smallish. The difference being, in a small town, everybody knows everybody. In a smallish town, you don't know everybody, but just about everyone you run into looks familiar. Which, most likely, they are — but you still don't *know* them.

That's the trouble I had with the new portrait. Hard as I tried to tell myself it wasn't important, I couldn't stop thinking about it. Glancing again at Sacred Heart as it pointed its holy head toward heaven, it crossed my mind that my mystery man might be a parishioner there. It was likely, actually, since I'd spent more time staring around at faces on Sunday mornings than paying attention to the pastor's sermons.

"Wait up, gravedigger!"

I groaned. *Not again.* Ignoring the voice, I pushed my shoulders back and continued walking. It was easy to pretend I hadn't heard Michael Romano. I was still angry at him for nearly landing his pogo stick on my feet and Mr. Finley's, and no way did I feel like telling him for the hundredth time, *My family doesn't actually dig the graves!*

"Wait up, Bernie! Who's the creepy guy staying at your house?"

That stopped me dead in my tracks, and I turned to face

Michael. At least he wasn't springing up and down this time. "How'd you know about Mr. Stein?" I asked.

"You're kidding me? Ha! Is that really his name? Mr. Stein. Let me guess. First name, Frank, middle name, Nathaniel? Right? Frank N. Stein. Get it? Frankenstein? Holy cannoli, you really are running a freak show over there at Alpine Monuments." Michael tipped his too-large head back and laughed.

I started walking again.

It didn't surprise me that Michael knew about Mr. Stein. Michael's an expert at getting into other people's business. He's what Mimi calls a "busybody," and I thought the word fit him in more ways than one. Not only was he a complete blabbermouth, he also couldn't seem to keep his body still (busy body, right?).

At that point, the steeple of Sacred Heart was piercing the sky just a block away. I hurried to put distance between me and Michael Romano. In some ways, *I guess* I felt sorry for him. He just wasn't a good fit for Stratwood. People around here liked things to stay the same as they'd always been. Same stores run by the same families. Same laid-back clothing styles paired with the same sensible shoes. Same restaurants with the same menus they'd been eating off for years. Same old everything.

Me and my family were enough of a departure from that "sameness" just by being in the business of making headstones. Michael was a full-on rattling disruption. His parents had been looking for a quieter way of life when they moved to Stratwood, but I'm not sure they realized they'd just be bringing the noise right along with them.

"Bernie, c'mon. You know I didn't mean it!" he yelled. The sidewalk was far from crowded, but the few people that were on it turned their heads to look.

I stopped. Not 'cause of Michael's apologizing. I wasn't embarrassed, either. It's just that my curiosity had finally gotten the better of me. "Where'd you see him?" I asked as I stood waiting for Michael to catch up.

"I didn't," Michael said when he'd caught his breath. "My mom did. Mr. Stein was wandering around Prospect Park yesterday." Prospect Park wasn't really much of park, more of a lake with some park benches and a trail around it. "You know how Mom is about loiterers," Michael added.

I nodded. Sheriff Romano kept Stratwood mostly free of all hitchhikers and other such riffraff. She must've gotten her fill of them patrolling the city before she moved here. I was certain the sight of Mr. Stein hanging around the park on a hot afternoon with his heavy overcoat didn't cause her any small thrill.

"He *claimed* he was staying with your family," Michael went on. "Mom let him go, but, knowing we're friends and all, she asked me about him when she got off her shift last night."

That was another annoying thing about Michael Romano. He thought everyone was his friend. "Well, you obviously don't know nothin' if you think we're friends," I shot back, still sore from his insults.

Michael kicked at a stick on the sidewalk and let his shaggy, dark hair fall down over his face. He almost looked like he felt bad for all the mean things he'd said and done to me. *Almost.*

Only a few weeks older than me, Michael stood a whole — in his case, large — head taller. Enough taller that I could see his dark eyes sparkle in the cave that was his hair. I could also see the smile he was trying to hide.

I glanced again at the church steeple. "Did your mom say anything else about *Abbot* Stein?" I said, emphasizing Mr. Stein's true first name. I thought Michael's mom must've spotted him soon after he slunk out of the carriage house. Probably right about the time I was guiding poor Mr. Finley back to his home on Benton Street. Hard to believe it had all just happened the day before.

"Nah. Nothing," Michael said.

"Right. See you later then."

"Wait, can I come with you?"

I didn't answer, but seeing how Michael kept following, it wasn't like I had much of a choice. He was still behind me as I pushed open the massive, hand-carved wooden doors of Sacred Heart. Sacred Heart, like a lot of churches, has a great deal of stonework and a whole bunch of statues. Things that, when I stand next to them, make me feel small and unimportant.

As we walked into the parish, our footsteps broke the silence of the sanctuary, and stained-glass saints frowned down on us from the windows above. We turned left, away from the worship space, and walked down the hall to the church office. The door was open, and I went right in. Michael trailed behind.

Mrs. Evans had her head down and was busily shuffling through papers on her desk.

"Wow," Michael said, looking around. Patchwork quilts and prints of cows and sheep were hung on the walls behind Mrs. Evans's desk, and tiny red hearts were plastered everywhere. "This place looks like a dairy farm."

I had to admit, the folksy decorations were a little at odds with the rest of the church, but Michael didn't have any business saying so. I threw my arm back, aiming for ribs, and landed my elbow in a tender spot on Michael's forearm instead. Michael yelped and rubbed at his sore muscle.

Mrs. Evans's head popped up. "Hi, Bernie! What a nice surprise to see you again so soon. And . . ." Her gaze shifted behind me.

"Michael," Michael said.

"Right. Michael. Sheriff Romano's son."

Mrs. Evans glanced back at me, and her smile radiated like the sun and warm apple pie all at once. I was relieved to see she wasn't holding any of my recent, unfriendly behavior against me, and I decided right then and there that if I ever felt up to sketching an older, plumper version of the Virgin Mary, I'd use her as a model.

"What can I help you with?" Mrs. Evans asked as she inched a bowl of Jolly Rancher candies in our direction. If her smile wasn't quite enough to brighten your day, she was always ready to sprinkle it with sugar.

I ignored the candy and held out the sheet of paper Dad had given me. We'd been running the same ad in Sacred Heart's weekly bulletin since Grandpa wrote one up over forty years ago. Now, on Dad's say-so, it was gonna change:

ALPINE MONUMENTS
GRANITE AND MARBLE CEMETERY MARKERS
FEATURING CUSTOM HAND-ETCHED PORTRAITS

Just as Mrs. Evans's fingers were about to curl around the paper, the phone rang, and she reached for the receiver instead.

"Just a minute, please," she said to Michael and me.

Michael nodded and snatched a watermelon-flavored candy from the bowl. Mrs. Evans winked at him.

I'd seen that wink before. A few weeks prior, she'd noticed the magazine I had tucked inside my Sunday missal. I thought for sure she'd rat me out to Mimi. Instead, she just grinned and winked at me before turning her attention back to the sermon.

"Hello. Sacred Heart Parish," Mrs. Evans sang into the receiver. She listened to whomever was speaking on the other end, and then, right before my eyes, her sunny smile crumbled to the floor. "That's terrible news," she said.

I perked up my ears, trying to figure out what could possibly have made her face drop like that.

"I see . . . Oh dear . . . When did this happen? . . . Yesterday afternoon at Prospect Park? My, how heartbreaking . . . Yes, we'll schedule the funeral for Saturday . . . I can't believe we're having another one so soon . . . I know. Sam Fuller's family must be devastated."

As Mrs. Evans spoke into the phone, giving the caller details for a funeral, an icy chill ran up my spine. "Where did your mom say she'd seen Mr. Stein?" I whispered to Michael. I already knew the answer, but I wanted to think I was wrong.

Michael narrowed his eyes. "By Prospect Park."

I dropped the ad on Mrs. Evans's desk and bolted for the door. I ran all ten blocks home, not slowing a bit the entire way. My heart raced and pounded in my chest, and I was panting like a dog by the time I reached the desk in the den where Mimi meets with all the grievers.

I pulled down a cheap metal picture frame from a collection lining the top shelf. I'd accidently broken a nicer porcelain one a few months before and had noticed then that a description was written on the back side of the photograph. But it hadn't crossed my mind to look at the picture itself — I mean really look — until Mrs. Evans's phone call shook something loose in my head.

I pulled the photo from its slot and flipped it over. Grandpa Morrison's shaky handwriting read:

Fishing with Sam Fuller

I turned the photo back over to its front side, and looked closely at the two old fishermen. Each was holding a string of dead-as-a-doornail rainbow trout. Grandpa was wearing an old blue cap with stick-straight brown hair poking out beneath. He also wore a smile that lived more in the eyes than the mouth — a smile just like mine.

The other guy, Sam, wore a broader smile, and . . . sure enough, bottle-thick glasses.

I'd been racking my brain this whole time, and, wouldn't you know, the photograph of the man from the portrait had been sitting on the shelf in the den all along. I still couldn't recall ever having met Mr. Fuller, but of course he'd looked familiar — seeing as how I'd been dusting over his face for years.

My thoughts started pulling together, but all it did was make me dizzy — the way I feel when I'm trying to solve a math problem and can't come up with the right answer. Everything I knew just didn't add up.

Mr. Stein was wandering around Prospect Park the day before.

Sam Fuller had died the day before *at* Prospect Park.

Sam's portrait was in the worktable drawer this morning.

I'd been around all evening yesterday, and all morning before I'd snuck into the carriage house, and I was certain Mr. Fuller's family had not requested a portrait.

Not yet, anyway.

Then there was the troubling speed, once again, with which Mr. Stein completed the portrait. Even if he'd started right after Mr. Fuller died and worked on it all night, I think he would've been hard-pressed to finish it by morning. Even then, I wasn't sure it could've been completed . . . Unless — what if he'd started it sooner? It's like he'd known that Sam Fuller was gonna die. What if —

Michael suddenly burst through the den door, "Where's the fire?" he said, messing up all the calculating going on in my head.

"What are you talking about?" I said. Why was Michael here? I wasn't thinking straight, and, of course, my question just set me up for another one of his stupid jokes.

Michael grinned. "As fast as you were running, I thought maybe your crematorium caught fire."

"Get lost Michael, before I cremate you."

"I just thought you might be interested in what Mrs. Evans had to say *after* you blazed out of her office. Guess not. I'll just get going. Catch you later, Grim Reaper."

He had me again, and he knew it. He wasn't budging an inch toward the door, regardless of what he'd said.

I huffed. "Oh, all right," I said. "What?"

"First, tell me what's going on."

I thought about it. I hardly wanted to talk to Michael about something as dull as the weather, let alone *this*. But the truth was, I needed someone to help me think things through, and I certainly didn't want to bother Dad or Mimi until I had a much clearer picture of just what was going on. So, as much as the thought irritated me, Michael appeared to be my best option. It took a little more hemming and hawing, but I finally decided that if Mr. Stein had something to do with Sam Fuller's death, the sheriff's son might just come in handy.

"Ugh. Fine. Here," I said, gritting my teeth and shoving the photograph at Michael. Then I told him about finding the etching in Mr. Stein's drawer, his frightening tools, and everything else.

Michael shook his from head side to side. "Man, this *is* one freaky place. I'd better get out of here before you wrap me in cloth and shove me in a sarcophagus."

I punched him hard in the arm, aiming for the sweet spot my elbow had connected with earlier.

"*Ouch*. You just gave my bruise a bruise."

"Just spill already, will you?" I said.

Michael rubbed at his arm. "Okay, okay. Sheesh. Mrs. Evans said Sam Fuller died of a heart attack yesterday afternoon at 3:30. He was fishing at Prospect Park when it happened."

"That's it?"

Michael nodded.

A heart attack? Well, that was disappointing. Of course, I should've known better. Michael's mom had seen Mr. Stein around the same time. I think she would've *noticed* if he'd been, say, covered in blood. Still . . .

"What was Mr. Stein doing there?" I asked.

"Don't know," Michael said, shaking his huge head. "But it's not like Mr. Stein could've *known* Sam was going to have heart attack. I mean, did he even know the guy?"

I threw up my hands and made a noise that came out sounding just shy of a horse snort. "So what was Sam's portrait doing in Mr. Stein's drawer this morning?"

Michael shrugged. I guess I didn't really expect him to have an answer.

"Well . . . I would've thought Mr. Stein would need days, if not weeks, to complete a portrait with *that* much detail . . . and Sam Fuller's wasn't the only one," I said, remembering how even Dad had been shocked by the speed with which Mr. Stein completed Mrs. Finley's portrait. "It's like he's doing the etchings before the people die."

I looked down at the floor. "That's not the way we do business," I said quietly, and then stopped. I expected another insult from Michael. When he said nothing, I went on, "Making a memorial for someone before they kick the bucket seems a little like burying a person alive."

Michael grinned. I could tell he liked the comparison. Especially since I was the one to make it. "Okay," he said. "So maybe Abbot Stein didn't *kill* Sam Fuller, but something majorly creepy is going on here."

I nodded my head slowly, not knowing whether to feel relieved that the stranger living in my backyard wasn't a murderer, or worried that he might be something worse.

"I want to see him," Michael blurted out.

"Are you nuts? We need to get help," I said. "Maybe your mom can arrest him or something?"

"Not a chance," said Michael. "Think about it, Bernie. As far as we know, the only thing the guy's guilty of is taking a walk near the place where Sam Fuller died of *natural causes* and, you know, being on the wrong side of normal. Half of the people in this town are a little wacko. Take you, for instance. Should my mom arrest you, too?"

I stared straight at Michael. There was no way I'd give him the satisfaction of rolling my eyes.

"Trust me. We can't tell anyone," he said. "Not yet. If Mr. Stein is up to something, we need proof." Michael put his hands on my arms.

I shook him off and took a deep breath. "*We?* As in, you and me?" Was this how it was going to be? Me and Michael working as a team? I'd almost rather face Mr. Stein alone.

Michael nodded.

Dang. But he was right.

I wasn't about to tell Mama what was going on, not in the state she was in. And Dad, Michael's mom, even Mimi — they wouldn't really believe it. I wasn't sure I believed it myself.

Maybe Mr. Stein was just a really fast etcher. Maybe it was all coincidence. Or maybe it wasn't even Sam Fuller's portrait in Mr. Stein's desk after all. Maybe it was just someone who looked like him. That's what Mimi and Dad and everyone else would say.

I thought I might even get in trouble for snooping if I mentioned it to anyone other than Michael. But I couldn't just sit back while Mr. Stein etched portraits that made my skin crawl and then nice people like Mrs. Finley and Sam Fuller wound up dead. What did Mr. Stein have against them, anyway? I hadn't a clue why he'd want them to die. As far as I knew, they were just . . . nice people. And what if Mr. Stein kept on etching his portraits, and even more nice people of Stratwood turned up as worm food?

Something had to be done, and Michael was probably the only person in town goofy enough to believe any of it, anyway. "Okay," I said after a long silent spell. "We'll go see him. But keep your big trap shut." I nodded toward the back door that led to the carriage house. "Let's go."

Michael smiled, showing both rows of his big white teeth. "Ladies first," he said, extending his hand out in front of me.

I snorted again and walked right past his bruised forearm and into the backyard. Instead of following the paver path, this time we crept close to the garage and back behind to the carriage house window. Michael and I bumped shoulders and then had a silent scuffle to see who would stand on the tile box first. Finally, we mounted the box together, side by side, letting our shoulders rub, which was far more than I, for one, was comfortable with. But at least that way we could peer in together.

"What's he doing?" Michael whispered.

"Dunno. Looks like he's getting ready to etch something," I said. Mr. Stein had his arms straight at his sides, like two steel rods. The hammer was in one hand, the chisel gripped firmly in the other. His head was tilted back so that his chin pointed like an arrow angled at the ceiling. His eyes were closed. He wasn't moving. On the worktable in front of him was a blank piece of black granite tile.

In a movement so swift I barely saw it, Mr. Stein's face dropped down and his arms swept forward. He pressed the chisel to the stone and struck the hammer with a force that was, at the same time, both soft and fierce. He reminded me of a conductor orchestrating a grand symphony.

Beside me, Michael gasped, and I lost my balance. I tumbled backward off the edge of the box.

Michael looped his hand under my arm and dragged me back up beside him. "Look! Look!" he whispered again. This time his voice was a few octaves above where it should be.

I did look. Mr. Stein's face was up, and he was staring straight ahead.

Then I saw what had Michael so worked up. His eyes! Mr. Stein's eyes seemed to be covered in a milky film. When I delivered the first tray, I thought Mr. Stein's gray eyes had seemed out of focus as he'd slid the tools into his pocket. They looked similar now, but not really the same. The white dullness was thicker, creamier, and horrifyingly strange.

"I don't think he can see us," Michael said.

Mr. Stein tilted his head in our direction and screwed up his face like he smelled a real bad smell.

"Maybe not, but he knows we're here. RUN!" I hissed.

Michael and I jumped down and scrambled for the garage. I was faster and crashed through the back door ahead of Michael. On the other side, I nearly bowled into my father.

"Bernie, what's wrong?" Dad asked just as Michael plowed through the door behind me. Dad looked back and forth between us. "You two look like you've seen a ghost."

I opened my mouth but clamped it shut again when I saw the expression on Michael's face. We still didn't have proof.

"Ahhhh, there you are." Michael and I both jumped at the raspy sound of Mr. Stein's voice behind us. "I'm afraid I might've frightened the children." Mr. Stein said to my father, laying out his hand in explanation. "You see, they startled me while I was working."

Slowly, I raised my eyes to Mr. Stein's. They were clear and gray — no trace of the milkiness anywhere.

"Working?" Dad narrowed his own eyes and his large brow creased into three straight lines. "We haven't had any other jobs come in that I'm aware of."

Exactly, I thought, *not even Sam Fuller's.*

The corners of Dad's mouth curled down. "Did Mimi . . ."

"Forgive me. What I meant to say was that I was working

on my craft. I find practice etchings very beneficial," said Mr. Stein.

My father nodded slowly. "Go on."

As shook up as I was, I couldn't wait to hear Mr. Stein's explanation, either.

"While I'm etching, I sometimes go into . . . something like a trance. It helps me do my very best work." Mr. Stein sneered at Michael and me. "The children found me in this state and I can only assume how alarming it must've been for them."

Despite my thudding heart and trembling knees screaming at me to run, I stood rooted to the ground. Dad would see right through Mr. Stein's story. I was certain of it. He couldn't possibly believe Mr. Stein worked in a trance, could he? Well, maybe that *is* what it was, but Dad wouldn't believe it was normal.

Dad shook his head, releasing all the folds and pleats from his face, and then let out a sigh. I think I heard him murmur the word *artists*, but I couldn't be sure. Then Dad did something I didn't expect. He aimed his misgivings right at us. Softer creases gathered around his eyes as he said, "Kids, you need to leave Mr. Stein alone. What were you doing back there, anyway?"

I couldn't believe it. To make matters worse, Michael was giving me a look that said, "See, what did I tell you?"

I ignored him and turned to face my father. "But Dad —"

"I think I can answer that," Mr. Stein interrupted. "She wants this."

Mr. Stein stepped between us and pulled the portrait of the beautiful woman out of his coat pocket. My heart thumped harder. He held it out to me. With his back to my father, Mr. Stein raised his eyebrows and said in a syrupy-sweet voice, "Here it is, Bernie. Go ahead. Take it."

"You don't need to do that, Mr. Stein. Bernie should know better than to be bothering you," my dad said, peering over Mr. Stein's shoulder at the woman's face.

"I insist," said Mr. Stein. Then, quieter, with a twinge of sadness that seemed to deaden his words, "I have no use for her anymore."

I snatched the granite piece from his hands. The jagged edges bit into my fingers, but regardless of all that had just happened, I was thankful to have it. With the portrait clutched to my chest, I did run this time. I quickly fled the room before Mr. Stein could change his mind.

CHAPTER
SIX

WHEN SAINT BERNADETTE WAS JUST A GIRL, A LOVELY LADY appeared to her. That lovely lady was the Blessed Mother. Not a whole lot of people believed Bernadette, but the reason she went on to became a brave, bold saint is 'cause she kept telling people about what happened. And then, of course, she also dug up a spring with miraculous water and had a body that never went to rot even after she was dead and buried. She still looked all fresh and young (and, in my mind, slightly creepy) when they opened her tomb years after her death.

Mimi thought it important I be named after such a courageous woman. It wasn't the first time, or the last, that her hopes were too high for me, and I rarely gave my namesake much thought. However, I couldn't help but think of Bernadette when I was visited by the beautiful woman from the portrait. I had to wonder if the saint ever felt like she was losing her mind, the way I felt I was losing mine.

Even if she had, my lovely lady wasn't the Mother of God (which probably gives one more clout), and since I didn't have plans to dig in the mud or be buried soon, I figured I was better off keeping the whole thing to myself. I may have dumbly given up all the other details to Michael, but I wouldn't share what I'd seen, or rather *who* I'd seen, standing at the foot of my bed.

The night before, I'd cradled the woman's portrait in my left hand as I worked on my sketch. I felt so confused. I didn't know what else to do. But, for the first time, drawing didn't seem to sooth me . . . nor did the portrait. The look on the lady's face was cheery enough, but something about the etching rang false. It was too perfect. There was nothing in her expression — her smile wasn't too tight, the sparkle in her eyes, too hollow — to make me think her joy in life had been unreal.

It was something about the masterfully etched lines scratched into the otherwise smoothly polished stone that roiled my stomach . . . and chilled my heart. The stone itself felt cold to the touch and, eerily, the coldness crept — inching from the palm of my hand, up my arm, through my chest — until it felt like icy fingers were grasping at, and then clenching, my heart. Whatever I'd felt from Mrs. Finley's portrait, it was nothing compared to this.

Yet for hours, I continued to sketch. I ignored the chill and the way the portrait numbed my fingers — I wanted so badly just to get it right. Part of me foolishly clung to the idea that everything would be okay. That I could make it okay. If I could just figure out how to make the portraits myself, I thought we could get rid of Mr. Stein and whatever sort of evil he'd brought along with him. And then things would get better.

But things were getting worse, not better. Or maybe things

were getting better for Dad, but certainly not for Sam Fuller and Mrs. Finley, and not quickly enough for Mama.

At last, the frosty feeling and the image I couldn't keep out of my head of Mr. Stein's milky eyes became too much. I gave up. I closed my sketch pad, placed it inside my nightstand drawer, next to the rolled-up drawing of me and Mama, and then set the granite portrait on top.

I climbed into bed and then folded the comforter down so it rested neatly below my knees. I used only a thin white sheet to cover my body. My mind told me it should be enough, considering the still-heavy heat in the air, and yet I couldn't stop shivering. I worried I was too shaken up to sleep, but exhaustion won over. As I drifted off, still shaking from the chills, I wondered if this was why Mr. Stein always wore that heavy overcoat.

Next thing I knew, I was dreaming about lying in a bed (which, incidentally, is never a good opening for a dream because it makes what is real and what isn't all fuzzy and blurred from the very beginning). Again, a smelting pot spewed fire in the darkness. I realized then that my bed was nothing more than a simple cot in the corner, and the floor of the room, dirt. On the cobblestone wall hung charcoal drawings: grotesque images that forced me to turn my head away. They were nothing like my own sketches. I always tried to capture life; these seemed to have the opposite intent.

Then a man stepped out of the shadows. His back was to the flame and he was holding something in each hand, though

I couldn't tell what in the dark. He moved forward again and moonlight fell through the window and lit his face. I could see a beard clinging to his chin like a furry marmot.

Suddenly, I was flat on my back in my own bed, and in place of the bearded man stood Mr. Stein. There were tools in his hands, moonlit and sharp — cutting the night with flashes of silver. He carried them toward me. I was frozen, unable to blink an eye, as Mr. Stein pressed the iron chisel to my chest, and raised the hammer high in the air — ready to strike.

I awoke with a scream in my throat and the feeling of cold metal on the skin just above my thumping heart. But that wasn't the most disturbing part. In that murky place between sleep and wakefulness, I saw her standing at the foot of my bed. The beautiful woman was not any part of my nightmare. She was in my room. My room — with its purple curtains and sea-foam-green walls. She was REAL.

I grabbed the portrait from my nightstand. It trembled in my shaking hands.

"Who are you?" I asked. But when I looked again she was gone, and in her place was only darkness.

I sat awake for the rest of the night, just staring at the woman's portrait, the memory of her apparition playing over and over in my mind. When the morning light finally came creeping in through the window, I quickly changed into a pair of jean shorts and layered a couple of tank tops. But even though the heat of the room had never left, and the day was set to be a scorcher, the chill of the night, and the portrait before that, lingered with me. Apparently, I couldn't strip off my night-mares as easily as I could my pajamas.

My knees felt wobbly as I stumbled down the hallway to Mama's door. I stopped outside. It was too early to bring in her tray, but Dad (who always rises before dawn) was sure to have left the room already.

I cracked the door open and slid inside.

Mama was asleep. I could hear her long, deep breaths, and I was thankful her night seemed to have been better than my own. I stood by her bedside, gazing down at her face. It was smooth. Her features didn't yet hold the ache of remembering, and I realized how badly I needed to see her like this. How badly I needed to see her at peace this morning.

Then my mama's lips parted, and she whispered my brother's name in her sleep. It came out full and sweetly heavy, her lips twitching up at the corners as she said it.

I winced.

Her dream wasn't plagued with smelting pots and cold, sharp chisels. She was having a pleasant dream about my brother, Thomas — named after Saint Thomas, of course. My brother who would forever be worthy of his saintly name, and *never* have it shortened to Tom or Tommy. I felt the sharp stab of jealousy.

Mama rolled over in her sleep, still wrapped warmly in her dreams of soft baby skin and dimpled chubby knees. It was time for me to leave. If she were to awaken while I was standing there, I'd have to watch as the truth came flooding back. I couldn't bear that.

Michael was sitting at the kitchen table chatting with Mimi when I finally made it downstairs. The sight of him threw me back a little, but I didn't know why. Seemed like everything happening lately was unexpected; what was one more surprise? I plopped down in the seat beside him.

Mimi clasped her hands together. "Oh my, I'll just carry this out for Mr. Stein." She hopped up and grabbed a tray stacked with blueberry pancakes. "So the two of you can have some time alone." Mimi leaned in close to me on her way out the door. "Nice family, the Romanos," she whispered.

I didn't even want to know what was going on in Mimi's head. She hadn't seen what I had. She knew nothing of Mr. Stein's milky eyes and strange behavior. Nor did she know enough to question the strange timing of Mrs. Finley's and Sam Fuller's portraits. She probably just saw Michael being here as some sort of old-fashioned courting. I shuddered. If any thought could be worse than the truth — that was it.

I slid a pancake onto my plate and busied myself sprinkling it with powdered sugar from a ceramic bowl shaped like a rooster. Next, I cut a bite off the pancake with my fork. It never made it to my mouth, though, 'cause as soon as Mimi left the room, Michael was grabbing at my arm. Blood raced to my face, and for a horrible second, I thought Mimi wasn't the only one who saw this as some sort of date.

"Don't even think about running," Michael hissed as he released my arm.

"What?" I dropped the fork and it clanked against my plate. For the first time since before we'd spied Mr. Stein etching or whatever it was he was doing in the carriage house, a smile almost reached my lips.

"Every time I see you, you bolt. I was scared, too, you know? You took off with that portrait and . . . and . . . I was worried about you." Michael's face was as straight as I'd ever seen it. Not a hint of humor anywhere.

I sat there just blinking for a moment. I wasn't sure what to think of Michael Romano looking so serious. But he was wrong. I wasn't thinking about running. I was thinking about telling him to get lost so I could eat my pancake in peace and move on from my nighttime nightmare to a more frightening, daytime one. One where I had to figure out what to do about Mr. Stein living in my backyard.

"Don't worry," I grumbled. "I'm not going anywhere."

"And?"

"And what?"

"Are you okay? Did Mr. Stein come after you, or what?"

I thought about my dream and shifted in my seat. "No," I said. "I'm fine."

Michael was still looking all tight-lipped and white in the face. He brushed my hand lightly with his fingers. I noticed his fingernails were clean, pink, and neatly clipped. Funny. I would've pegged him for a dirt-under-the-nails kind of guy.

I slid my fingers back. Couldn't he just tell a joke or jab me with one of his insults? The last thing I needed was for him to be acting all nice.

"Don't mind me," Mimi sang into the kitchen. "I just need to grab a dishcloth. Sloshed a little orange juice, see?" The way Mimi was beaming at the two of us, I was certain she'd seen the hand brushing but had not caught anything else.

I shoved a bite of pancake in my mouth, and Mimi, after retrieving the cloth hanging by the sink, left the room again.

"Is there somewhere around here we can talk?" Michael said, watching my grandmother leave.

I shook my head. "Dad and Mimi will be walking through all day." And even though I didn't mention it, there was no way he was coming up to my room. Mimi may have liked him and all, but she would undoubtedly draw the line at that.

"We'll go to my place, then. Mom's on shift. She won't be home until late this afternoon."

I nodded and took another bite of pancake. The soft, squishy blueberry inside warmed my mouth, but nothing else. Considering the shivers still running through me, I didn't much feel like arguing with Michael. "Okay." This time I carefully set my fork down beside my plate.

We both rose from the kitchen table. "Wait right here," I said. Since I finally had the woman's portrait in my possession, the last thing I wanted to do was leave it behind. By the time I returned to the kitchen with it tucked inside my school bag, Mimi was back from delivering Mr. Stein's breakfast.

She looked me up and down from behind her spectacles, and I felt myself waver under her glare. Could Mimi see the dark fear that had planted itself in my heart and had been growing there ever since Mr. Stein moved in?

"Don't worry about the lunch trays or cleaning up the showroom today, Bernie. I can take care of it all myself," she said, apparently finished with the fine-tooth combing she'd been giving me with her eyes. "You look a little pale. And tired. Maybe I've been working you too hard. I'm sure you could use a day off with a . . . friend."

Dumping my chores on her, in addition to all she had to do, wasn't exactly part of the plan for bringing my family back together, but I had more pressing concerns. "Thanks, Mimi," I said. "You're right, I could."

Michael bounced his toes on the floor and kept glancing at the pogo stick leaning against his dresser. I guess you could call it progress. As annoying as his jiggling was, at least he was sitting down.

We didn't fully buy the trance story or that the timing of Sam Fuller's portrait had been a coincidence. But it didn't take long to realize neither of us was gonna come up with anything short of a Brothers Grimm fairy tale. And I hadn't even mentioned the lady appearing in my room at the crack of dawn.

I sat stiffly on the yellow-and-orange striped comforter draped sloppily over Michael's bed. (I had to give him credit, though, for at least *trying* to make it.) Sitting across from me in a chair, Michael went from bouncing his knees to drumming his fingers on a small wooden desktop. I looked carefully at his hand again. This time I noticed not only his clean fingernails, but his long, wide fingers as well — they seemed almost out of proportion on his skinny wrist. Like five fat popsicles on a single stick. I don't know why, but I imagined sketching them.

Michael noticed me watching, and I quickly turned my head away, moving my gaze around his room instead. He seemed to like his stuff like he liked his life — busy. There was a marble track on the floor, a model airplane on the desk behind him, photographs of buildings and architectural drawings all over the walls, one of those scientific weather barometers, a chessboard, and a whole load of other stuff I didn't recognize. Still, as much stuff as there was, it seemed more or less organized.

I stood up from my place at the end of the bed, stepped over a rogue pair of boxer shorts that looked like they might've accidently slipped out of his dresser (a sight I immediately tried to erase from my memory) and walked over to a row of photo frames on his headboard. Michael riding a roller coaster . . . Michael outside a large sports arena . . . Michael on a baseball team. Moving to Stratwood, where the biggest event was a farmers' market in the middle of town, must've been really rough. No wonder he thought springing around on a pogo stick was a good idea. He had to come up with *something* to do.

I picked up a photo of a spunky-looking girl in a cheerleading uniform. "Your girlfriend?" I asked.

Michael burst into a sudden, tear-spilling belly roll of a laugh. I stood waiting. Just like with his eruption of laughter upon jumping out from behind one of the backyard headstones, I was not nearly as amused. Finally, he gathered himself enough to say, "That's my *cousin*, Giovanna."

Cousins always seemed liked a good idea to me, maybe 'cause I didn't have any. "You two close?" I asked.

That sent Michael into another fit of laughter. "Giovanna's only close to herself. She gave me that photo as a Christmas present."

"I see your point."

"And she lives in Silverton, so I don't see her much," Michael added.

"Silverton?"

"Uh-huh, why?"

"That's where Mr. Stein said he was from."

Michael stood up now, too, all traces of laughter gone from his face. "Oh yeah? Why didn't you say so? C'mon."

Michael's house was quiet as we stepped into the hallway. No humming sandblasting machine, no one bustling around in the kitchen, either. Michael said he had three older brothers, but they stayed behind in the city, and his dad traveled back and forth between the two for business. I imagine, except for when Michael's blabbermouth filled it with noise, his home was pretty peaceful.

As I followed Michael to the study down the hall, I noticed I'd finally sloughed off the chills. A feeling of warmth seemed to come not from the air, but from family photos on the wall and a board game on the coffee table. From a long-haired cat curled up on the couch purring softly and three pairs of running shoes lined up by the front door. There was clutter, for sure, but it was the happy-making kind.

Inside the study, Michael reached up to open the cabinet above a massive oak desk. I stood close to him as he pulled on the brass knob. He smelled like a mixture of soap and freshly peeled oranges. *He smelled nice.* I frowned at myself for thinking so.

Michael withdrew a phone book.

"Why do you have the yellow pages for Silverton?" I asked, shaking off whatever had come over me.

Michael looked at me with his big, dark eyes. "My mom's a cop, remember? So is Giovanna's dad. Crime does cross city lines from time to time."

Michael flipped to the section for Ss.

"Give it to me," I said. "Don't you even know how to use a phone book? These are business listings. Not personal ones." I turned to the M page looking for monument companies. There was a slight chance that if Mr. Stein had really worked for one, his name would appear somewhere on an advertisement.

"There's none here," I said, disappointed.

"What about that one?" Michael pointed to an ad for National Insurance on the opposite page.

"I hardly think Mr. Stein worked for an insurance company," I said, starting to close the book.

"Then what's his name doing there?" Michael held the book open and pressed his fat finger down on a line of the ad I hadn't seen before. Sure enough, Abbot Stein was listed as the local insurance agent for National Insurance.

"Nah. Who'd buy life insurance from a man who looks like a murderer himself?" I said. "It's gotta be a different Mr. Stein."

"We could call the number and ask," said Michael.

"Yeah, and what are you gonna say? 'Hey, are you the scary man living in the Morrisons' carriage house who etches headstone portraits with lightning speed?'"

Michael shrugged and picked up the phone to dial. After six or seven rings, he set it back down. "Answering machine."

"What did I tell you?"

"Maybe he didn't *answer* because he *is* living in your backyard instead of in Silverton."

"Yeah, or maybe the guy's just out for lunch." I looked at the hands on the old-fashioned clock hanging on the wall, both pointing straight up. "I should take off."

Michael gave me a look that was half hurt, half confused. "Mimi said you didn't have to be back for lunch-tray duty."

"It's not that . . ." I said. I didn't want to explain what a rare thing it was for me to have an afternoon off. And I certainly didn't want him to know how I was planning to spend it.

"Well," said Michael. His big-footed sneaker twisted back

and forth on the carpet. *Was he nervous or something?* "Can I walk you, wherever it is you're going?" he spat out at last.

"Heck, no," I said, more out of reflex than anything. Then, when I saw the hurt on his face grow, I added, "Maybe next time, okay? I just want to be alone right now."

Michael nodded. He was still looking glum when he saw me to the front door and carefully shut it behind me. For a second, I almost felt guilty. Then I remembered this was Michael Romano we were talking about. Why should I feel bad about disappointing him?

CHAPTER
SEVEN

THERE'S A CERTAIN KIND OF CHARM TO A CEMETERY. THE trees are tall and strong — no weak young saplings you can't depend upon for shade. The grass is green and cut weekly. And it's quiet. Always quiet. The perfect place for thinking.

The older monuments sit on a hill along the back side of Stratwood cemetery. They were placed there long before Grandpa started the family headstone business. I could just barely make out the split pillars, crooked crosses, and concrete angels sinking into the ground from where I was standing. The newer ones, those sold by our very own Alpine Monuments, were set in neat rows — standing straight and proud. But, to be honest, the warmth from Michael's house had worn off, and I was feeling more like the old headstones — cracked and sinking under the weight of it all.

Yes, this thing all started with Mr. Stein, and, of course, I didn't like him none. But there was more to it than that. Stuff I didn't understand. I knew Mr. Stein was etching portraits in some bizarre manner that seemed connected to the deaths of Mrs. Finley and Sam Fuller and possibly even the woman from the portrait, but how? And was it really Mr. Stein that ran a chill so deep down my spine? A chill so cold I could feel it even with the sun directly overhead. Maybe it wasn't Mr. Stein. Maybe it was simply Death himself.

I knew people probably thought Death was a friend to the Morrison family, bringing us so much business and all. But really, our family had been chewed up and spit out by it more than most. We knew all too well how Death, like Mr. Stein, could be an unwanted guest — rarely seen, but a dark presence just the same. A darkness my mama could never seem to shake.

I moved easily through the sea of headstones, as I knew my way well, finally stopping at our family monument. Grandpa picked it out decades ago, the very week he started Alpine Monuments. He thought that being the owners of the local monument company and all, we should have the most impressive monument in the cemetery.

And it is.

It stood at least a foot taller than the rest and twice as large — large enough to someday honor the entire family. Two inscriptions so far . . . Plenty of polished stone just waiting for more gray lines to be carved out like ditches in the jet-black granite. I'd often wished Grandpa had picked something in green or pink instead of black — you know, to soften the blow. Make Death seem more colorful. Even if it isn't.

I glanced at the two names on the stone and tried to keep my focus on what was above the ground, instead of below. Suddenly I didn't feel like standing or thinking anymore, so I took a seat on a cement bench at a nearby grave site. I sat there awhile, watching the trees sway in the breeze. Smelling the dampness of the fresh-cut grass and listening to the hum of the afternoon traffic helped me forget about everything else.

"Bernie?"

I flinched when Michael spoke my name.

"Are you okay?"

My surprise quickly turned to anger. "Michael Romano!" I narrowed my eyes at him. "What are you doing here? Did you follow me?"

Michael shrugged. Looking not at all shamefaced, he took a seat beside me on the bench.

I inched away from him. "How dare you spy on me!"

"Like you would never spy on anyone? Not even Mr. Stein?"

I huffed and looked the other direction.

Michael looked around, too, finally resting his eyes on the dates on my family's marker. "How's your mom doing?" he said softly, after a spell. Like I said before, Michael's always poking himself into other people's business.

I thought about lying to him, but he'd been at my house just a few hours before, and Mama had been as scarce as always. He had to have noticed, and I was pretty sure he'd know if I didn't say something that at least resembled the truth. "Not good." I sighed. "It's been weeks since she's come out of that tomb of hers." More like months, I thought to myself.

"I'm sorry," Michael said. He sounded like he meant it. "Maybe she'll be better after, you know . . ."

I looked back at the dates now, too, and like Michael,

focused on the one just a few weeks away. But I knew better than to hope. Hope was something that almost never came through for my family. "Yeah, maybe," I said, not wanting to think about Thomas. But with his grave marker staring us in the face, his death was hard to ignore. I swallowed hard and shook my head; it was a trick I'd learned to help keep back the tears.

Michael slid closer to me on the bench. Close enough that his arm was touching mine and his fine, dark hairs tickled the skin on my own arm. I felt it again. What I'd felt at his home. *Warmth.*

"He was two months old," I blurted out. Maybe I needed a distraction from whatever it was Michael was making me feel, or maybe I just had too much piling up inside. I had to let some of it loose. I might burst if I didn't. "My mama wanted a house full of children. Instead, she got me," I said, and then laughed without any humor behind it.

Michael didn't laugh. He just waited for me to go on.

I opened my mouth again, and even more leaked out. "Right after my first birthday, Mimi and Grandpa Morrison moved out to the carriage house thinking they'd make room in the main house for another baby," I explained. "Years went by, but no baby came. That's when Mama started to get sad. Then Grandpa died and Mimi moved back in with us. Alone."

Michael looked at the marker again, this time at the dates beneath my grandfather's name. "How'd your grandpa die?"

I shrugged. "Mimi said it was a combination of old age and too much bacon."

"Oh," Michael said. He squirmed a little but stayed put. Most boys I knew would've come up with excuses and taken off already, but not Michael.

"I was pretty young. Don't hardly remember it happening."

Michael turned his face back toward mine. "And your brother?" he asked hesitantly.

I made myself swallow again and pushed against the sob bubbling in my throat. "After Grandpa passed away, Mama kept trying to get pregnant. It even happened a few times, but they didn't take. I always knew when she'd lost another baby, 'cause she'd stay in bed, crying like she does now."

Michael dropped his eyes from mine and looked down at the grass.

"Mama would come out of her room when the tears ran dry, and for a while, she'd pretend like nothing was wrong. But I knew something was missing. I knew I wasn't enough to keep her happy. You know what I mean?"

A weak smile blossomed on Michael's lips — an "I'm sorry" without the words. I'd forgotten he had three brothers. He couldn't possibly understand.

"Anyway," I said. "When she finally got pregnant with Thomas, she stopped crying, and she didn't sit in her room all day." I couldn't believe I was saying all this (to Michael Romano of all people!), but I didn't stop. Sitting in the cemetery — all too close to the tiny coffin — made it impossible to tuck it away, back to a safe, rarely visited corner of my heart.

"Mama was amazing after Thomas was born," I said. "She sang these silly songs while she folded laundry and danced when she filled Thomas's bottles."

The sob in my throat began to taste sour with guilt as I remembered those precious few weeks. I didn't tell Michael how jealous I'd been that Thomas could turn my mama into this happy person when I couldn't. How her delight with each coo and goofy grin had felt like an insult . . . even though I knew it shouldn't. Nor did I tell Michael the dark fear I had. The fear that some small part of me, unsaintly me, had wanted the terrible thing that happened next.

I took in a big gulp of air, trying to calm myself, or maybe shut myself up, but I didn't succeed at either. "Then, about a year ago . . ." I nodded at the headstone and continued. "When Mama went to wake Thomas from his nap, she started whimpering and moaning, and she didn't stop . . . Hasn't really ever since." I paused for a second and then added, "It happens sometimes, babies not waking up."

I risked a glance at Michael's face. He looked like, for once in his life, he didn't know what to say. To him, the cemetery was probably just a spooky place to avoid on Halloween. Not a place to visit loved ones. Not a place that punched you hard in the gut and then apologized with peace, quiet, and the sweet smell of grass. No. Right about now, Michael was probably wishing he'd never followed me here. And I was starting to feel glad he had. I felt lighter somehow. I'd said a lot, and it was nice of him to listen.

I moved my face closer to his and stared until he looked me in the eye. Side by side like we were, our noses were nearly rubbing. I whispered. "Do you think there's any point, Michael? I mean, why are we bothering with Mr. Stein at all? What difference is it gonna make? We can't prove anything. And we can't stop him . . . or Death . . . or whatever this is." I dropped my gaze to the wild blades of grass growing like vines around the legs of the cement bench. The ones the mower couldn't reach.

"Maybe we can't," Michael said, and I lifted my eyes back to meet his.

"But maybe we can," he added. "At least, I think we should give it a shot. Don't you?"

I thought about that for a moment and then nodded my head.

Then another thought occurred to me. "Why are you helping me?" I asked. It wasn't like Michael had a madman creating portraits, or signs of death — whatever they were — in *his* backyard. If he wanted, Michael could leave me alone and go about his summer without giving it a second thought.

Michael gave me a funny smile. A crooked smile. And the way his eyes sparkled, despite their dark color, made my stomach lurch. Then, before I knew what was happening, he was bringing his face in even closer to mine.

My wanting heart gave a quick flutter. My stomach flip-flopped again. I started to lean in slightly, too. My own eyelids were half closed before I finally came to my senses and pushed him away. I pushed him hard — probably a lot harder than he deserved. Michael landed with a soft thud on the ground behind the bench, and his eyes popped open.

"Disgusting!" I said. "Did you just try to kiss me?"

"Umm . . . Yes?" Michael said.

"Are. You. Kidding. Me. Michael Romano? In a cemetery? What's *wrong* with you? I'm thankful for your help and all, but I do *not* want to kiss you. *Got it?*"

Michael looked down in his lap. "Okay."

"Ugh," I mumbled, and then said, "I guess I should thank you."

"What for?" Michael asked.

"For reminding me why I don't like you."

Michael leaned back on the grass where he'd fallen, crossed his legs, and pulled his hands behind his monstrous head like a pillow.

I shook my own head, and then added another "disgusting" for good measure. But this time, what was barely a giggle slipped out with it. I pinched my lips tightly together, but it was too late. Michael had heard the giggle and the good humor behind it. He smiled. I turned away quickly so that my own thin smile was hidden as I walked away.

CHAPTER EIGHT

AFTER ANOTHER NIGHT OF FRIGHT-FILLED DREAMS, AND after I'd shooed Michael out of the house (he'd arrived in time again for breakfast, like a stray cat looking for milk), Sara Fuller showed up in our den. Sam Fuller's daughter was about my mama's age. She wore a dark, freshly pressed business suit that seemed at war with the blond, scraggly ponytail, lopsided on the left side of her head. I noticed, too, how Sara's eyelids were rimmed with color, like someone had taken a red crayon and drawn her suffering in around the eyes.

When she spoke, her voice was that of someone forcing their words to walk a narrow line, knowing one small slipup would send them wavering out of control. "We saw this in the new bulletin and we were thinking a hand-etched portrait of Daddy might be nice," she said. She held out a copy of the ad I'd delivered to Mrs. Evans. It was clenched so tightly between her fingertips, it seemed as though she was trying to dissolve it there.

Luckily, Mimi was with me in the den this time. She guided Sara to the same padded chair Mr. Finley had collapsed in, and then pulled her own chair from behind the desk and sidled it up close to Sara's.

Now, I already knew that Sam Fuller's family hadn't placed an order for his portrait yet — the one finished and waiting in Mr. Stein's drawer — but seeing it all play out in front of me was unreal. Like watching a scary movie. One where you're screaming at the pretty actress to watch out, but knowing the whole time there ain't no way she can hear you. I could hardly scream at Sara and Mimi. But the feeling was the same: helplessness.

"Mr. Stein does lovely work. Perfect for our dear Sam." Mimi's face mirrored Sara's heartache. I hadn't even thought about Mimi being upset over the death of Sam, him being a friend of Grandpa's and all. I took a step toward her. Mimi gave me a weak smile and continued, "What about a granite tile insert, honey? Abbot can engrave the portrait, and we can inset the stone in something like . . . A blue pearl monument would be nice."

Feeling as low-down as I did, I could only manage to let out a tiny gasp of air. The portrait of Sam I'd seen was on a black tile, one I'd wager was swiped from the tile box behind the carriage house window. And now, Mimi was helping out Mr. Stein by selling the very portrait he'd already engraved — only neither Mimi nor Sara knew it. I just couldn't stomach anymore.

If I'd been thinking more clearly, I would've grabbed them both by the hand and dragged them to the carriage house. I would've beat down the door and shown them Sam's portrait already made, and then let Mr. Stein try and explain that one.

But at the time, I didn't fully appreciate how dangerous the portraits were. And who knows, the unexpected sight of her father's face immortalized in stone might've been even harder on Sara. Either way, I didn't. I just ran past Mimi and Sara Fuller. I ran through the kitchen and up the stairs with the loudest thunking-clunking footsteps I ever made.

"Bernie?" My father poked his head out of his and Mama's room just as I reached the landing.

With my already mixed-up emotions, I nearly burst at the sight of him. Here Dad was, doing just what I'd wanted him to do all along. Apparently, with Mr. Stein around, he'd finally found some time to pay a little attention to Mama. But it wasn't right. It just wasn't right. Not with Sara Fuller and her messed-up hair and puffy eyes downstairs. I wanted my mama dragged back into the land of the living, but not at Sara's, or anyone else's, expense.

I hardly looked at Dad as I sprinted past him and into my bedroom. I pulled back my purple curtains and glared down on the carriage house, wishing it would simply explode into a fountain of flames with Mr. Stein in it. What was he up to out there? Working on another portrait? Would his etching mean another life stolen? Another kindly person, like Sara's father or Mr. Finley's wife? Was a life ending at that very moment with the tap-tap of his hammer and the chip-chipping of his chisel?

I was so caught up in my anger and frustration that I didn't hear Mimi come in. "Is everything all right, Bernie?"

"It's just . . . Mr. Stein . . . He . . ." *I didn't know how to say it all.*

"Ah, yes. Abbot. He told me he may have startled you."

"What?"

"I delivered his trays yesterday, remember? So you could go off gallivanting with Michael. Well, we sat and talked for a spell and I fear I may have misjudged him."

"No," I said. And then a second time, putting more heave into it, "*No!*"

"Now, Bernie, you should know better than anyone what misery can do to a person. When Thomas, well . . ." Mimi's eyes shifted down the hall in the direction of Mama's room. "I know Abbot can seem strange . . . frightening, even. But I think he's just real torn up inside over Isabella's death. The whole thing's just heartbreaking if you ask me."

I shook my head back and forth. "Wait. Who's Isabella?" I said. I'd been about to come clean and blurt everything out to Mimi, but that was all suddenly derailed.

"Why, I was sure Abbot told you. He didn't mention her when he gave you her portrait?"

I glanced at the sheet of granite resting on my nightstand, thought of the shimmering image I'd seen at the foot of my bed, and began piecing things together. "Isabella? I mean, no. I didn't know her name."

"I don't know the whole story myself," Mimi said stuffily, "and I sure wasn't going to pry. But by the way he described her . . . and the work he put into that etching . . . Well, it seems to me he was madly in love with her." Mimi's eyes went soft and misty.

I didn't put much stock in what Mimi was saying. She thought everyone should be in love. Just look at the tickled way she eyed me and Michael together.

"Oh, and don't worry, Abbot said he's already working on another portrait of Isabella." She glanced at the one on my nightstand. "Although, I don't think it's quite right — you keeping the first after the spying you were doing. Abbot said he caught you peering in the window at him while he was working on it." Mimi finished what she was saying and then made a show of bunching her lips together disapprovingly.

"Yes, but —"

Mimi put her hands up. "I know, I know, I'm somewhat to blame. By not wanting him in this house, I certainly gave the impression he couldn't be trusted. But I never meant for you to spy. Troubled or not, I believe Abbot's harmless. He may even be a right blessing on this family. So I'm telling you now, there will be no more peeking in his window. For heaven's sake, Bernie!"

"But, Mimi —"

Mimi clicked her tongue loudly and the stern look on her face sharpened. I turned my gaze to the floor and nodded my head slowly. Once Mimi's mind was made up, there was no changing it.

"Good. Then tell me, how was your day with Michael?" Mimi's tone changed in an instant and her thin gray eyebrows rose above the top rim of her glasses.

I groaned inwardly. "Nice?" I said just to please her. I couldn't very well tell her about the extra digging we'd done into Mr. Stein's past, now could I? Or even about the time Michael and I had spent together in the cemetery. What would she think of *that* as a first date? Me babbling on about our family's miserable past and then knocking him off the bench when he'd tried to kiss me . . . My face filled with heat thinking about it. However, my flushed skin just seemed to make Mimi's eyes twinkle all the more. "I thought so."

Mimi sighed and her lips pulled back down at the corners, "Well, I'd better get back to Sara. But you remember what I said about Abbot. You leave that poor man alone."

"Mimi?" I said, trying to muster up some courage before she left. Maybe I could approach it a different way. "What do you know about signs . . . um . . . I mean the kind that predict something's gonna happen . . . something bad?"

Mimi's frown deepened. "What kind of bad, Bernie?"

I took a deep breath and let it out. "Signs of death coming." I'd given it more thought, and it was as close to an answer for what Mr. Stein's portraits were as I could come up with.

"Now, Bernie. You know the only signs I believe in come from above. So unless God is speaking to you from a burning bush, I say you forget all about them."

I nodded and smiled as best I could. There was no sense in discussing things further with Mimi, not with the stern look lingering on her face from the mere mention of the topic. I could only imagine what she'd think if I told her Mr. Stein was etching them. Especially after the cozy chat they'd apparently shared the day before.

All of a sudden, Mimi's eyes widened and her nostrils flared. "Are you mixed up in something you shouldn't be? One of them boards that tells you stuff, or those cards?"

"No. *No!*" I said, fighting once again to make Mimi believe me. However, as hard as I pleaded with my eyes to make it crack, Mimi's face remained like stone. "It's nothing. *Really*," I said, and smiled brightly. "I was just curious what you thought."

Mimi's lips bunched together again, and she turned and walked out of my room without saying another word.

I exhaled heavily just as soon as she was gone. Trying to talk to my grandmother had obviously backfired, and how was I supposed to bring it all up to Dad? His mood was finally on an upswing and he was visiting Mama. I couldn't possibly be responsible for crushing his spirits now.

I raised the phone and turned to the only person I could. "Hey, Michael," I said when he picked up on the other end.

Michael answered cheerfully. "Bernie, is that you? You just can't get enough of me, can you, Grim Reaper?"

"Shut that hole in your big head and listen to me. I know the woman's name."

I thought about sketching after I got off the phone, but my insides were knotted in a ball and I couldn't seem to sit still. I decided it would be best to return downstairs. Was it too much to hope that Sara and Mimi would be looking through sandblasting designs, having forgotten all about hand-etched portraits? Most definitely.

The order for Sam's portrait sat on Mimi's desk, as heavy and alarming to me as an eviction notice. Mimi was smiling benignly, sitting on one side of Sara, and Mrs. Evans had joined the condolence party, sitting on the other. The three women had their fingers intertwined like ropes. Some of the color from Sara's red-rimmed eyes seemed to have found its way back to her cheeks. I was glad.

I pictured myself pushing in and then locking my fingers between Sara's and Mimi's. But if I tried, I knew I wouldn't be welcomed into their circle, at least not at the moment. The contrast between the gentle softness Mimi's face held for these women and the hardness it had shown upstairs in my bedroom just a few minutes prior said it all.

Feeling hopelessly left out, I scuttled past and quickly found things to busy myself with on the far side of the showroom. A short while later, Mrs. Evans walked up behind me and cupped my elbow in her hand. "Bernie?" she said.

I glanced behind her. I hadn't noticed when Sara left. Mimi was out of sight, as well. Most likely she'd made off for the kitchen to ready the lunch trays.

"Yeah?" I said. "Are you headed up to see Mama?"

"In a bit . . . but I wanted to ask you something first." Mrs. Evans's eyes crinkled around the edges. She looked at me much more fondly than I deserved, and I wriggled in her grasp and away from her adoring gaze.

Mrs. Evans didn't seem to notice my discomfort, or else she overlooked it. "Mr. Finley told me how kindly you treated him the other day. It takes a special heart to show that kind of compassion. Bernie, I . . . I was wondering if you'd like to join the outreach committee I'm putting together."

"Me?" I nearly spat. Hadn't she seen the way I'd ignored her outside Mr. Finley's house? I wasn't good with people, not like Mimi was. Even if she hadn't figured that out already, the look on my face had to be making it clear — but if anything, Mrs. Evans's smile only grew wider.

"Thank you," I said, somewhat belatedly remembering some of the manners I was raised with. "But I don't think I'm what you're looking for."

"Give it some thought, Bernie." My answer didn't faze her any more than my wriggling had. "Our first meeting is next Sunday after mass," she continued. "We'll gather outside the worship space, and then visit community members. People like Mr. Finley whose lives can be brightened by small acts of kindness."

"Dad and Mimi need me around here to take care of things," I retorted. It was the truth, and in my opinion, a pretty darn good excuse, as well.

"Mimi's already given her blessing. She thinks some time away from here might be good for you, dear."

So that's what this was all about. It was just a ruse. Luckily I hadn't fooled myself into believing that someone like Mrs. Evans could actually find me as kind and caring as she was making me out to be. The sting would've hurt a lot worse if I had.

No. After our conversation earlier, Mimi was worried about me. Not Mr. Stein. But yours truly. Thinking I was headed down a darkened path, what with my spying and asking about creepy signs, Mimi had sent Mrs. Evans to fluff me up and straighten me out like a wrinkled pillow case.

It was all I could do to remember this was Mimi's doing, and to keep my tone pleasant as I answered, "Okay. I'll think about it and let you know."

"I know you'll enjoy it, Bernie. If you give it a try."

I started to speak, but Mrs. Evans stopped me. "Just stop by the office in a few days and let me know, all right?"

I nodded, mostly to get rid of her.

As soon as Mrs. Evans left, I stormed into the kitchen. Just as I'd suspected, Mimi was finishing up the lunch trays and I snatched Mr. Stein's right out from under her. I fumed as I carried it to the carriage house door, knocked, and then, in spite of Mimi's warning (or maybe in part because of it) slipped around the back side.

There was no real use peeking in the window, but that's not why I was there. I'd been thinking about something while I was working on my chores, while Mimi and Mrs. Evans were consoling Sara . . . And, incredibly, that something was bugging me even more than Mimi's meddling.

Sure enough, when I slipped open the corrugated, cardboard lid, the box of granite tiles was half empty. There'd been a box of twelve to start, and now there were only six tiles left. I counted one of the missing tiles for Mrs. Finley, one for Sam Fuller, and one to replace the tile of Isabella — if Mr. Stein had been telling the truth about making another one — that left three or four more missing tiles.

Or were the tiles already engraved, dark and dangerous threats tucked inside the worktable drawer? But why? Why would Mr. Stein want to do this? I wondered if he'd truly loved Isabella as Mimi suggested. A great love lost could bring madness upon just about anybody, or so I'd heard.

If only Mimi had listened to me. Where would Mrs. Evans's small acts of kindness and her own rank if she knew the people of Stratwood were gonna keep dropping like flies? The anger stirred again inside me. Was this what drove Mr. Stein to strike the stones with his sharpened chisel? Was it anger that drove him, or a deep, aching chill? Burning with annoyance myself, and yet cold with fear, I stood there shivering and quaking in the hot July sun. More deaths were on the horizon. I could feel it in my bones.

CHAPTER
NINE

FOR THE NEXT FEW DAYS, THE SUN CONTINUED TO FIX ITS fiery eye on Stratwood. The roofs of cars sizzled in the heat and the pavement surrendered, going all soft and rubbery beneath the soles of my shoes. Everywhere I looked, foreheads were lined with beads of sweat, and shirts were pitted out and stained. Yet the sun couldn't seem to find me. I lived in the shadows, in a cool, dark place the sun couldn't break through.

I thought about trying to talk to Mimi again, but every time I came close to doing it, I'd think about the conversation she must've had with Mrs. Evans. One of those I-don't-know-why-that-girl-can't-keep-her-nose-out-of-trouble talks I so often inspired. And then I'd think about Mrs. Evans offering up a spot on her outreach committee as a wholesome activity, and I just couldn't go through with it. At the slightest hint of darkness, I was pretty sure Mimi would start researching at what age I could enter a convent.

So instead, three times a day, I dropped off a full tray at the carriage house and picked up an empty one. And three times a day, standing with my ear pressed to Mr. Stein's door, I listened to the sound of stone being chiseled and scraped, and fought the urge to confront him. It wasn't a lack of wanting that stopped me; it was the not-knowing-how part. And doing nothing was worse than anything.

Dad was still visiting Mama, and I didn't want to do anything to jinx that; but, nonetheless, her outbursts were getting louder and louder as the dreaded anniversary neared. Rather than being high-pitched and shrill (which might've been easier to endure), her cries were deep and low and seemed to come from some hollow place inside her. She hid her face each time I entered her room, and her body heaved with sobs beneath the sheets. I struggled to come up with something to say, anything to soothe her sadness. But just like Mr. Stein's evildoings, Mama's heartache seemed to stretch far beyond my reach.

Then one morning I passed Dad as I walked down the stairs. He rounded an eyebrow into a question mark, but kept walking. In the kitchen sat Michael looking even livelier than usual. Leave it to Dad to make a quick exit and let Mimi handle the mystery of the boy who'd become a regular at our breakfast table.

For her part, Mimi didn't seem to see any mystery in it at all. She just seemed thrilled by Michael's reappearances and was whistling "Amazing Grace" as she scrubbed dishes in the sink. With her back to me, and with Michael's head buried in a stack of chocolate-chip pancakes, I was able to stare at him all I wanted. With his dark, flopping-down hair and a smear of chocolate to match on his chin, I was pleasantly reminded that there were still lighthearted and fun things in the world.

"Did you leave any for me?" I kidded as I slid into the seat beside him.

Michael shrugged his shoulders and a grin spread across his face. "Nope. But you can have a bite of mine." He cut a piece with his fork and shoved it at my mouth.

I ducked away from his hand and threw a napkin at him. "Just wipe the chocolate off your face, would ya?" I said.

Mimi stopped whistling and chuckled softly. Then she picked up a tray from the counter and said, "I'll just take this out for you, Bernie."

"Thanks, Mimi," Michael and I said together. As soon as she'd left, Michael's face twisted into a funny expression I couldn't quite read. "There's something I've got to show you. I left it at my house."

Michael dropped an issue of the *Silverton News* on the desk in front of me. "You found her!" I said. I think if someone would've held a microphone up to my brain just then, they could've heard all the clunking and chattering going on inside as I scanned the article with Isabella's photo next to it. "How'd you get this?" I asked.

"You remember my cousin Giovanna from Silverton, right?" Michael said, flipping the newspaper back a few pages. "Well, there she is."

Sure enough, the perky-looking cheerleader from the frame on his nightstand was pictured in a full-color, whirly pirouette of a pose on the front of the sports page.

"Her team took state and finished third at nationals. If you'd rather read about them, be my guest."

I took the paper from him and folded it back to the story about the woman from my portrait. "No, thank you," I said curtly. "But you still didn't answer my question. This paper's from June twenty-ninth, two weeks before Mr. Stein came a-strutting in my front door. What've you been doing, holding on to it this whole time? Why didn't you tell me you had a Silverton newspaper?"

"I didn't tell you because I haven't been holding on to it. I called up Giovanna *after* we found Mr. Stein's name in the Silverton yellow pages."

"You told her!" I said. "You told *me* not to tell anyone, but then *you* went and blabbed it all to your cousin?" Of course he did, I thought angrily. Michael's mouth would have to be taped shut for him to keep quiet. And it would take a great deal of duct tape considering how big his dang head was.

"I didn't tell her nothing," Michael grumbled. "Except how I thought she should send those newspapers she's always bragging about. Told her I didn't believe she'd ever been in a single one. Lucky for us the *Silverton News* has been running a column on Giovanna's team, highlighting their trip to nationals. She sent all of them and I read through two months of newspapers to find this one." Michael tapped his finger on the picture of Isabella.

"Oh." I felt slightly ashamed for jumping to conclusions and decided to let Michael keep full movement of his mouth . . .

for the time being, anyway. "Thanks. That was a good idea," I said quietly. "Now shush, so I can read."

> Isabella Freemont, heir to the Freemont Foundation, was found dead this morning when firefighters responded to a three-alarm call at her residence. However, officials do not believe fire was the cause of death.

I felt the pulling-down weight of Isabella's portrait in my backpack. (I carried her everywhere with me these days.) I knew she was dead, but somehow reading about it made it seem more real.

> The county coroner found evidence Ms. Freemont suffered a heart attack preceding the flames that ripped through her home Wednesday. It is still under investigation as to whether or not the fire was deliberately set. Authorities speculate the fire may be related to a break-in reported by Ms. Freemont weeks prior. If you have any information regarding the fire or the burglary, please contact Rocco Romano of the Silverton PD.

Michael sat there, smiling proudly and waiting for my reaction.

"Okay," I said at last. "Let me guess, Giovanna's not the

only relative the town of Silverton found newsworthy? Rocco Romano, he's related to you, too, somehow?"

"Uh-huh. He's my uncle." Michael cocked his eyebrows at me.

I thought for a moment. My brain clunked and chattered some more. Isabella died of a heart attack, just like Mrs. Finley and Sam Fuller. All three of them seemed to have met an unfortunate, untimely death. But what of the fire, and the break-in, too? It wasn't like this paper had cleared anything up. There was still a load of unanswered things about Isabella, so why was Michael acting so full of himself?

"*You* think he'll help us," I said.

Michael nodded, still grinning, and his eyebrows arched even higher — ridiculously high.

"Aren't ongoing investigations closed to the public?" I asked. "Even if he is your uncle, he's not gonna want *us* poking around in police business."

"True, but the police can't resist sharing their cases with fellow officers of the law, in this case *a sister-in-law*. Get it? She's his sister-in-law and a sister . . . in . . . law."

I groaned. Michael may have grown on me. Slightly. But his jokes had not. In fact, the dose I'd had that morning was just about enough already. "Your mom? No way. We're not dragging her into this now." I crossed my arms in front of me. "You said so yourself. She won't believe it."

"What won't I believe?" Mrs. Romano popped into the doorway to Michael's room. Her long brown hair was slicked back in a knot, looking like a cinnamon roll at the base of her neck. Her uniform was fitted and crisp, and a dark metal gun peeked out from the holster on her hip.

I swallowed a lump the size of a chestnut.

Michael quickly flipped the newspaper back to the sports section with Giovanna's picture front and center. "Mom!" he said. "Hey, did you get off early?"

Sheriff Romano looked back and forth between Michael and me. "Nope. I'm still on duty. I picked up an extra shift tonight. But, with your father out of town, I thought I'd swing by to check on you. Now, what won't I believe?" She rested her hands on her slender waist. I stared at the long fingertips on her right hand — the ones resting just above her firearm. I knew what Mimi would do with a gun if she found a boy in my bedroom.

"That I want to go visit Cousin Giovanna in Silverton," Michael said.

"You're right. I don't. Giovanna loathes you."

"Actually the word she used last Christmas, after I laughed at the photo she gave me of herself, was *detest* as in, 'Michael Romano, I *detest* you.' Then she said I was more repulsive than the slime between a toad's toes. I tried to tell her that was impossible since toads don't actually have toes, you know, because of the webbing and all, but —"

"Enough, Michael. Just get to the point already. What possible reason could you have for wanting to see her?" Sheriff Romano asked.

"I don't want to see her. Bernie does."

"What?!?" I shrieked. I'd been listening closely to see where Michael was heading with all this, but I wasn't even half expecting he'd turn it back on me.

"It's okay, Bernie," Michael said, holding on to my angry stare with a teasing one. "She won't tell anyone." Michael turned back to his mother, "You see, Mom, Bernie really wants to try out for cheerleading when school starts up again, but she doesn't want anyone to know."

I shook my head and then stopped abruptly. Any denying. I did at this point was only gonna make Michael's stupid story seem all the more true.

"You know how girls are, Mom." Michael rolled his eyes for effect. "Bernie's scared she won't make the team. So she's embarrassed. But Giovanna *is* captain of Silverton High's cheerleading squad, and they even went to nationals. Remember how she kept going on and on about it last time we visited, and I told her to keep on talking and maybe one day she'd say something interesting?"

Michael paused like he expected us to laugh. When we didn't, he cleared his throat and went on. Michael was good at talking. "Anyway, Bernie was hoping I could introduce them so she could get some pointers to help her with tryouts. What do you think?"

Mrs. Romano narrowed her eyes. I was certain she could taste the thick lie that hung in the air. Isn't that what police officers do? But then her face softened and her lips curled up in a smile. "Well, I wouldn't mind catching up with Rocco and Celeste. Maybe we can drive down on Sunday after mass."

Michael grinned widely and held his hand up, palm out, in front of me.

I shrugged and slapped Michael's outstretched hand. Not because I wanted to, but because I needed Mrs. Romano to think I was actually excited about going.

Michael's mom let out a huge, long sigh and said, "Michael, I don't know what I'm going to do with you."

"That makes two of us," I said.

After Mrs. Romano left the room (like Mimi, chuckling as she went), I turned to face Michael. "Cheerleading? C'mon, really, Michael? Cheerleading? I don't know the first thing about *cheerleading*. How on earth am I going to pretend I have a clue when I meet your cousin?"

"Don't worry, Bernie," Michael said. "Just say the word *cheer squad* and Giovanna won't shut up. You'll be schooled on everything from basket tosses to car washes in no time."

"Basket tosses?"

"Just trust me."

"Right." How was I supposed to trust someone who thought *cheer squad* was one word? Plus, I wasn't convinced going to Silverton was such a great idea in the first place. If Michael's family knew something sinister about Mr. Stein, wouldn't there be an all-points bulletin out for his arrest? I was afraid, too, that if we went to Silverton, all we'd find would be more suffering. And I didn't know why we should go looking for more when we already had plenty enough here to go around.

Michael picked up the phone to call his relatives and let them know we were coming. After a few rings, I heard him say, "Hello, Giovanna," into the receiver. He said it the way you hear a TV superhero greet his nemesis. Or did I have that backward?

Just then, I remembered what else was going on after Sunday's mass. "Oops. I gotta go," I said. I glanced back at Michael as I left the room. He had this exaggerated grimace on his face that made me want to laugh. When his pained looked changed to one of confusion, I added, "I'll explain later." I wanted to get to Sacred Heart before Mrs. Evans took her lunch break. I still hadn't given her my answer.

CHAPTER
TEN

THE MOMENT I PUSHED THROUGH THE HEAVY DOORS, I KNEW something was wrong. I knew it from the tingle on the back of my neck and from the nagging echo of my footsteps as I treaded lightly as I could down the marble hallway. I could tell something was wrong at Sacred Heart Parish the same way I could tell when a house was empty, or when someone was lurking in the shadows. I could feel it.

The door to Mrs. Evans's office was open and I slipped inside.

When I saw her, I wanted to think she was just bent over in prayer. The way I find Mimi sometimes — peaceful and closed off to the world. But when she didn't respond . . . when I touched her arm lying stretched out on the desk, and it felt cold — colder than any living arm should be — I knew.

Mrs. Evans was dead.

Maybe I shouldn't have been quite so shocked. Maybe I should've seen something like this coming. I couldn't have possibly believed that Mr. Stein would stick to people that I only kind of, sort of, knew. But it caught me way off guard nonetheless. Death always does.

I thought to myself, *I really should be screaming*. I couldn't, though. I couldn't make a sound. My mouth hung open. Ready. But my heart was too busy shattering for me to let loose the wail stuck in my throat.

When something finally did shift aside and the noise was able to claw its way to the surface, it escaped my mouth in one long, shrill "Noooooooooooo." So trilling and animal-like was the sound that I didn't even recognize it as my own. The sound was eerie enough to call Father John out of the chapel to investigate (when not many things could), and it didn't stop until he grabbed me by the shoulders and shook.

"Enough, Bernie! I have to phone for help, and I need you to be quiet so they can hear me."

I *was* quiet then. Deathly so. I waited and watched in silence as the paramedics arrived, as Mrs. Evans's vital signs were taken, and as shaking heads passed on what was obvious. I waited and watched as her body was covered with a sheet and — like a ship's billowed-out sail — was rolled away.

I think questions were asked of me. I know they were. I had fuzzy images in my head of faces appearing in front of me and mouths moving, and of my arm being gently squeezed once, maybe twice. Then I was alone.

How different I felt walking out of Sacred Heart Parish than before I'd walked in. I'd left Michael's feeling stubborn. Feeling blown up with my grand reason for telling Mrs. Evans I couldn't join her dumb outreach committee. How quickly things could change. Why hadn't I learned that already?

Back outside, the sun was still hot. The air, still dry. The smell of charcoal and sizzling red meat wafted over from the grill across the street. On the sidewalk, people (most of whom I recognized) had bunched together. They must've been drawn to Sacred Heart by the bright spinning lights and roaring sirens; the silence the emergency vehicles were now leaving in had to seem equally as blaring. The small crowd stood frozen to the pavement as the county coroner pulled her car away from the curb.

I looked at them. And they looked back at me curiously, whispering among themselves, "What happened? Who was it? What's going on?"

Then my tired eyes rested on a figure standing away from the group in his black overcoat, and I noticed the way his head hung down while everyone else stood perched on tiptoes.

I clenched my fists tight, my knuckles turning as pale as the sheet on Mrs. Evans's gurney. My fingernails cut into the skin on my palms. *He* didn't have to stretch and strain to see what was going on. He didn't have to listen to the whispers of the small crowd.

Mr. Stein already knew.

I took off running like never before. People, houses, cars, everything was a blur until I reached the carriage house. I jimmied the window latch again and slithered through the opening. I yanked the drawer on the worktable and pulled it entirely off its tracks. *CLANG. BANG.* The heavy drawer rattled as it slammed to the floor.

One by one, I lifted granite tiles from the stack inside. Then I swung each tile high up in the air and smashed it down on the side of the worktable, not stopping to think it through. Lightning-like cracks splintered the faces etched in stone, and the pieces crashed down, clattering and spinning across the carriage house floor.

It felt good.

I felt a surge of power race through me with each smashing of stone . . . until I reached the last one in the drawer.

I'd expected to find Mrs. Evans's portrait there; any lingering doubts had vanished as soon as I saw Mr. Stein standing on the street outside the parish. But I wasn't prepared for what holding it in my hands would truly be like.

My knees nearly buckled. I glanced down at the shattered pieces of stone lying on the floor and they stared back at me accusingly. Ghost-gray eyes, turned-up noses, receding hair lines, smiling teeth — all shattered apart.

I lifted Mrs. Evans's face, looking so happy and full of life — nothing at all like the way I'd just seen her — and used the worktable to shatter her portrait, too. I couldn't stop myself — not with horror and anger exploding like fireworks inside me.

The worst of it was the guilt. I could've tried harder to make Mimi listen to me, I knew I could've. But I was too busy being upset with her for her meddling. And Dad? It was so selfish of me to think his good mood was more important than this. Mrs. Evans was dead. I might've been able to stop it, but instead I'd done practically nothing. Sure, I'd told Michael and we'd had a few conversations, but *that* wasn't enough. It didn't matter what I did, it was *never* enough.

"I take it you weren't as fond of these portraits as you are of Isabella's."

I jumped high and fast, spooked. More than I'd ever been in my whole life. My heart, beating hard from the running, from the anger and the smashing, threatened to punch itself right out of my chest. And there was Mr. Stein standing before me, as calm and cool as a mountain lake.

Mr. Stein. To have made it back so quickly, he must've run, too. But even in his overcoat, he hadn't broken a sweat. And, during my wild fit of destruction, I hadn't heard him come in. I took a step back, positioning myself closer to the open window behind me.

Mr. Stein's jaw, as usual, was rigid, but in his eyes was a look I couldn't quite place. I thought it must be a twinkle of smugness, a look of pride, but that's just what as I was expecting to see. In reality, his eyes were moist, clouded.

Then he took a step — a dreaded step closer — and the moistness in his eyes turned to ice. He reexamined the sea of sharp, jagged pieces I'd created, and the look he gave me was one of pure hatred — evil all the way through.

I lifted my foot and angled my body away from Mr. Stein, but before I could take my chances and split out the back window, Mimi stepped through the open door of the carriage house. "What on earth happened here? Bernie, did you do all this?"

She must've heard the ruckus. I didn't know whether to

run to her arms or scream for her to turn and run away. It didn't make any difference, 'cause before I could do or say anything, Mimi saw all the anger and shock, the guilt and sorrow, painted in bright colors on my face and took that for her answer. "I don't know what gets into you sometimes, Bernie. Really, I don't," she said angrily. "First peeking in the window and now this?"

I pointed my finger accusingly at Mr. Stein, hoping Mimi would forget about me looking guilty as sin once she saw the murder and madness in his eyes. But, by then, Mr. Stein had dropped the devilish look. He just seemed distraught and shrunken inside his black overcoat and was doing a fine job of appearing the victim in all this. (In his mind, maybe he was.)

Mimi turned back to me and put her own finger to her temple, applying pressure as if to ease a growing migraine. If she'd been upset with me for spying on Mr. Stein, she was as mad as a whole hornet's nest now.

I glanced down at the floor at all the shattered, unrecognizable portraits, and then I bit back at both Mimi and Mr. Stein with my glare. Honestly, I didn't know what had gotten into me, either. Not in the way Mimi thought, but because I'd just destroyed all the evidence. How could I've been so stupid? I knew more people were gonna die. The proof of it lay broken at my feet. My rage had taken over, and now I had nothing. Nothing to prove Mr. Stein was the guilty one, the one responsible for all this death and darkness.

It occurred to me then, from the way Mimi was standing

with her arms now crossed and her face pinched, and from the way she'd responded with such a force of anger, that she hadn't heard the news. News like this traveled quickly in Stratwood, but surprisingly I had beaten it home. "Mrs. Evans — she's dead," I said flatly.

I flew past Mr. Stein and reached Mimi about the time she crumbled. I caught her by the arms and held on as she let out a moan to rival one of Mama's.

For the moment, everything else was forgotten. The broken portraits. Mr. Stein. The fact that I'd just ruined my best shot at proving something horribly twisted was going on with the etchings. All I felt was the grief passing between Mimi and me as I hugged her thin and trembling body.

Somehow we found our way out of the carriage house and to the kitchen table. I told her all about finding Mrs. Evans, cold like she was. Then we huddled together, remembering, but not talking. Mrs. Evans had been so kind to our family ever since Thomas died. Who was gonna deliver care baskets now? Baskets delivered by anyone else would seem empty — no matter how full they were.

I stayed with Mimi for a while. She didn't question what had happened out in the carriage house again. Grief-stricken as she was, I don't think she had enough spirit left over for anger. She cried. I didn't.

Sweet, kind, Jolly Rancher–pushing Mrs. Evans was gone, and strangely, I wasn't aching with sadness anymore. I wasn't feeling helpless or scared, either. All of which I should've been.

I just felt numb.

When Mimi's tears finally trickled dry, I asked her if she thought it spooky, all the people dying lately. Mimi just said, "When you get to be my age, Bernie, so many people you know start passing away. You have to check the obituaries each morning to make sure you aren't one of them."

I think she was trying to lighten the mood, but it just made things worse. What if Mimi *was* next, or Dad, or even Mama? I had destroyed everything in his drawer, but what if Mr. Stein was working on a new portrait that very minute?

Mimi finally stood up from the table and started rustling around in the cupboards. She would bake something — cookies, bread, maybe a lasagna to bring over to Mr. Evans. That's how she'd move on from this. As she was pulling out a pan and fretting out loud about whether or not to tell Mama the horrible news, I slipped back outside.

There were still six tiles left in the box beneath Mr. Stein's window. I tried to remember just how many portraits I'd broken, and I thought there were four, counting Mrs. Evans's, which meant all the tiles were accounted for. To say I was relieved was as large an understatement as saying I didn't like Mr. Stein.

I hauled the box and blank tiles with me back into the garage, found a sledgehammer, and — well — it didn't take long for the remaining six tiles to be smashed to bits, too.

I was sweeping up when Dad wandered in. He rubbed his hands together and then laced his fingers, as if in prayer, before studying the mess and the look on my face. I could tell he was uncomfortable without his goggles on or the blare of the sand-blasting machine to fill the space between us.

Dad cleared his throat. "About Mrs. Evans," he said quietly as he released his hands and then fiddled with a button on his shirt. "Mimi just told me." He cleared his throat again and his eyes traveled down to the broken chips and pieces of black tile scattered across the floor and in the dustpan. "Are you doing okay, Bernie? Are you feeling all right?"

"Yeah," I lied. I knew both he and Mimi would expect me to be in some sort of shock or something. It's not every day you happen upon a dead body — especially one whose life meant something to you. Sure, I'd seen them before, at funerals and viewings, and I'd never get over the image of Thomas's still body lying in his tiny white casket, but finding one on your own was different. And, truthfully, I didn't know what I was supposed to be feeling.

Dad nodded his head and looked like he was about to amble off like the giant bear that he was. He'd done his job. He'd checked on his only daughter who'd just witnessed something awful. But then he surprised me and said, "Did I ever tell you I wrecked an upright monument after Thomas died?"

I shook my head, afraid that if I spoke, he might stop.

"It feels good to destroy things when you're hurt and angry, doesn't it?" He didn't wait for me to answer. He just made a hollow noise that seemed like a chuckle but wasn't. "I had to buy a new sledgehammer and everything — tore the head off the old one, cracking it against the stone."

I pictured my dad releasing his anger on a piece of rock the size of a human. But then my father said something that really got to me. "It's a good thing when you're hot inside — to take it out on something that will break, but that you can't do any real damage by wrecking. Something like those tiles. As long as you're careful" — Dad paused and reached for his safety glasses before handing them to me — "no harm can come from chipping rock."

As it turned out, Mimi decided not to tell Mama about Mrs. Evans, and I sure as heck wasn't going to. But that didn't stop me from imagining it.

When I delivered Mama's supper tray that evening, I stood over her, willing her to look at me . . . not *through* me. I imagined what it would be like to have a mama who wasn't sick with sadness, or maybe just my mama back the way she'd been when we were sketched together at the county fair.

I'd tell her what happened and about Mrs. Evans's cold, cold arm. Then my mama would hold me and stroke the unruly hairs away from my face, and when she looked at me, it would be in the eye, and she'd absorb some of the hurt she saw there. But my real mama, the one who rarely made it out of bed, didn't have the room to absorb any more pain.

So when she did turn her face toward mine, I shielded my eyes from her so that she couldn't see all that was there. The hurt. The want. The numbness that was beginning to transform into something else entirely. Fear.

"Enjoy your dinner," I said, and quietly left.

I usually saved delivering Mama's meal for last, but I'd wanted to put off visiting the carriage house for as long as I possibly could. Forever would've been nice. My plan was to drop the tray off and slip away unnoticed, but before I could, Mr. Stein threw the door open quickly with a wry smile on his face.

I desperately wanted to expose him for the evil man that he was, and I wanted him to answer for the wrongs that he'd done, but I had no idea just how wide and far and deep the blackness of his heart could reach. Were the portraits even important? Had I smashed the tiles for nothing? Could he simply wish anyone dead, and then it would be so? I was utterly and fearfully at his mercy. Any words I might've spoken fizzled and died in my throat.

"Looks tantalizing," Mr. Stein said. He retrieved his dinner tray and then shut the door softly in my face. I picked up the tray containing the leftovers of his lunch and walked away in a daze. Halfway across the yard, the tray slipped from my hands and landed flat on the ground in front of me. Remnants of a pork chop bounced from the plate and onto the ground, and a half-empty glass of milk toppled over and began flooding what remained of a pile of peas. I didn't take any steps to correct it.

Dad must've been watching out the window and sensed something was wrong, 'cause right away, he rushed out, righted the glass, and picked up Mr. Stein's dirty tray, all without saying a word. He waited for me to come back from standing on the edge of terror, and then he followed me inside to deliver the tray to the kitchen himself.

For the next few days, I dragged my body around the house like it was too much for my bones to carry. Mimi took notice of how I didn't talk to anyone, the way I slumped everywhere, and how the simplest of duties ran me plumb out of energy. Even though she was dealing with her own pain, she lightened my chore load.

I'd like to say I used the extra time to plot against Mr. Stein, that at the very least, I figured out a way to convince Dad and Mimi to get rid of him. I didn't, though. Mostly I sat in my room dreading the sound of the phone ringing or the doorbell buzzing. I feared either one would only bring more bad news. What concerned me the most was that all of the victims (other than Isabella) had been connected to my family in one way or another. Were we somehow luring the victims in for him?

Who would be next? I was betting it would be someone else I knew. Possibly even someone truly close to me. As if I hadn't punished myself enough feeling guilty over Mrs. Evans's death, I was now obsessed with the people in the other portraits. If I knew who they were, and if by some miracle they were still alive, could I somehow throw a monkey wrench in the works? Could I stop their deaths from coming?

I hated myself for not really paying attention to the other faces as I smashed their portraits to bits. I was too focused on finding Mrs. Evans's portrait (not to mention blinded by fury) to think of anything or anyone else. But there was this one image . . . The shadowy memory of it haunted me even more than the rest. What if . . . ? No, it was too horrible to think.

I also sketched. Of course, I sketched. The point of it this time wasn't to ease my guilt or to bring me some small relief, though. And I wasn't foolish enough to pretend that learning how to do hand etchings was still in the slightest bit important — not in light of everything else going on. No, I sketched like mad trying to re-create the destroyed portraits on my pad. But it was no use. The faces hadn't fully imprinted themselves on my brain in the few seconds before I'd destroyed them. And it felt tragic that they hadn't.

I did remember having the impression that not all the etchings were complete as I swung them through the air and struck them hard on the side of the table. In fact, I recalled that some of them, or at least one in particular, was really just a rough outline of a person.

Once I'd exhausted myself tugging every last detail I could out of my brain and then putting it onto paper, I carried my drawing pad down to the den. I knew it was a long shot, but I figured if Mr. Stein had plucked one of his targets right out of a photograph behind Mimi's desk, he might try it again. Not surprisingly, none of the features I had to go off seemed to match those of the people in our photographs, and I just got spooked while I was down there, anyway.

As I held my wretched drawings up next to Mimi's photo frames, Mr. Stein walked in the back door. I immediately dropped the pad and my gaze, but he leered at me until I finally raised my eyes to meet his. Then, certain I was paying attention, he poked his head through the archway and into the garage. My stomach leaped into my throat as he very loudly said, "Jonathan, mind if I trouble you for some more granite tiles?"

I had one last pitiful idea for identifying Mr. Stein's other victims. I waited until the night before garbage pickup, then took a flashlight down to the end of the drive. While everyone else was (hopefully) sleeping, I dug the heaviest bag out of the can. I stretched and tore the plastic until the side ripped open and the broken pieces of granite fell to the cement with a quiet clatter.

I wish I could say it was like putting together the pieces of a puzzle, but it was much, much harder. There were all these tiny shards that didn't seem to fit anywhere. Plus, not only was I trying to fit four different portraits back together, all the tiles I'd smashed — including the blank ones — had wound up in the same garbage bag. And did I mention it was nighttime and that I couldn't see very well even with the flashlight? (It might've had something to do with the fact that I was trembling so bad, I couldn't hold it steady.)

At least the whole thing confirmed that my impression had been right. Some of the etched lines were indeed so vague that even if I could've told whether I was holding a man's or a woman's chin and which nose it belonged with, it wouldn't have mattered. The portraits didn't seem to be far enough along that I actually could've identified familiar faces, even if I somehow managed to put all the pieces back together. It was hopelessly impossible.

Just as I was giving up and was sweeping the jagged pieces back into a pile with my hands (wishing I'd also brought out a broom), I pricked my finger on a sharp, pointed edge.

I knelt down to get a closer look. I'd been hunting for facial features (thinking they'd be the easiest to identify), so I must've ignored this piece until it jumped out of the pile and bit me. The etching on it resembled a hand, and although the minor details had not been chiseled in, something about the fingers seemed youthful. I dropped the flashlight. It landed heavily, but the sound it made seemed far away.

No, no, no, no, no, nooooooo! PLEASE, no! I picked up the light and shone it on the piece. I ran my finger across the granite scarred by Mr. Stein's chisel marks and tried to wipe away the drop of my blood that now smeared it. My worst fears were true. The etching was of a very familiar hand, and the odd proportions of it were unmistakable. Five fat popsicles on a stick.

"Oh, God. Please, no. Not Michael!" I whimpered in prayer and in shock.

I nearly lost it. I nearly became just one more broken thing in the garbage that surrounded me. The only thing that kept me from turning into one big, blubbery mess that would still be gasping for air and sobbing when the trashman came in the morning was knowing that if I did, I'd never be able to save my friend.

CHAPTER TWELVE

IF MICHAEL HADN'T SOMEHOW MANAGED TO WRIGGLE HIS way into my life in the first place, he never would've fallen into Mr. Stein's crosshairs. So when he showed up just after the garbage truck in the morning, I made Mimi turn him away at the door. I wouldn't answer any of his phone calls, either — all seven of them. If I could make Mr. Stein think I'd forgotten all about Michael Romano, maybe he would forget about him, too. It was a long shot, but it was all I had. Besides, I thought Michael would be better off without me, anyway.

All I ever did was make things harder on those around me. And discovering part of Michael's incomplete portrait proved that I needed to handle things alone. I'd push Michael away, and I wouldn't tell anyone else about Mr. Stein. I couldn't be responsible for causing any more harm or danger than I already had.

By Saturday morning, Michael still hadn't taken the hint, so I met him myself at the door. The hugely relieved smile he greeted me with made it impossible to look at his face. "I'm not going to Silverton with you tomorrow," I mumbled, unable to let my gaze fall anywhere but on his giant, scuffed-up shoes.

I could tell by his feet that he wasn't taking the news well.

They shuffled and shifted around on the ground until finally he said, "But, Bernie, you have to!"

Taking a deep breath, I glanced up slightly. His hands. The sight of them and how clearly I'd been right about them being the ones in the etching chilled my heart. I dropped my gaze back down to his shoes. "I can't," I said, nearly choking on those two short words.

"Bernie?"

The way he said my name — so tender with hurt — completely sunk me. I didn't want to back down, especially when I'd just resolved to go it alone. But even though I didn't think we'd find much in Silverton, and I worried it wasn't worth the risk, I hadn't been able to come up with anything else. I had to give it a shot, and I needed Michael to do so. At least in Silverton, we'd be far away from Mr. Stein. It had to be safer for him there than it was here, right?

I peered around one of Michael's shoulders and then the other. The street behind him was clear. "Okay," I whispered, "I'll go, but you're not coming in for breakfast." Then I quickly shut the door before he could say my name again and make me change my mind on that, too.

Mimi and I sat two rows behind Michael and his mother on Sunday. I nervously scanned the crowd, but not a single churchgoer was wearing an overcoat — wise choice since a normal person would have probably sweated to death in the heat.

After the final blessing, Father John announced Mrs. Evans's rosary service. It was scheduled for Thursday evening followed by her funeral and burial on Friday. As Father John spoke of the arrangements, Michael rubbed his eyes. It might've been that a bead of sweat was running down his forehead and he was merely wiping it away, but I tend to think he was remembering Mrs. Evans's wink and watermelon candy, and that he was hurting for her, too.

After mass, Mimi walked me outside to where Michael and his mom were waiting by their car. We wouldn't be riding to Silverton in a police cruiser as I'd secretly hoped (something about riding in a police car made the journey seem far more protected), but in Mrs. Romano's beat-up green Jeep Cherokee instead.

Mrs. Romano leaned against her old SUV and discussed the funeral reception with Mimi. She planned on bringing spaghetti, and Mimi would bring Dad's favorite, barbecue meat loaf. Michael stared at me the whole while. I gazed up at the purple-and-red stained glass windows on the steeple so I wouldn't have to meet his eyes. I thought about how if Mrs. Evans were still alive, a small group would be meeting nearby. I also thought about all the poor community people who would be missing out on her kindness that day, and every day thereafter.

Finally, Mimi grabbed my hand and gave it a squeeze. Mass — which had seemed so long it felt like it would darn near kill me if I didn't die from the heat first — always did have a way of putting *her* in a better mood. I climbed into the back of the Jeep. Michael and his mother climbed in the front.

Mrs. Romano turned to smile at me before twisting the key in the ignition. I smiled back. Michael turned around and smiled, too. I waved out the side window at Mimi. I still couldn't look at Michael. Not with the secret I was keeping, aching to pop.

I'd learned my lesson in the cemetery: Michael had a way of making me talk. Maybe it was his endlessly dark eyes. They'd sucked me in like two black holes, untied my tongue, and made it flap it around carelessly. I'd said too much about Mama and Thomas. But a funny thing happens when you share a hidden part of yourself and the person you share it with doesn't laugh or quietly excuse themselves and then take off, full sprint. You start to care about that person.

I cared about Michael. A lot. I might not like admitting it to myself, but I did. As we drove away, I said a silent prayer for his life and for Stratwood to have the exact same population count when we returned.

After ten minutes of Michael maneuvering his head around the seat, trying to catch my eye, he finally seemed to take the hint that I didn't want to look at him, let alone talk. He spent the rest of the car ride fiddling with the radio — tuning in new channels as we lost others to static. Mrs. Romano asked about my summer and if I was looking forward to school starting next month. "Summer's good," I said (a lie). "And school, no" (the truth). She stopped asking questions after that. I guess she'd left her interrogation skills behind, along with her police cruiser and her gun.

Mostly, I watched the passing view outside the car window. The road to Silverton was winding and, for the most part, the land beside it was building-bare. One single highway connected the two towns with spurts of cabins and other one-gas-station towns in between. Everything else was what Mimi called "God's canvas."

The aspen trees were ripe with green leaves and they tore through the denser, darker pines in light-colored patches. Every now and then I'd catch sight of a trickle of water running down a hillside — proof that the tip-tops of the mountains were still spiked with snow, even this late in July.

The farther we got from Stratwood, the brighter the sun seemed to shine and the lighter my heart began to feel. It was good to get away. It felt like we'd slipped beyond the reach of Mr. Stein's chisel markings. Michael was alive and well in the seat in front of me, and I could actually do something as simple as breathing without looking over my shoulder. By the time we arrived in Silverton, everything going on back home had the feel of one of my nightmares — real and horrifying, but escapable.

Anyone could tell just by the looks of it that Silverton brought in more tourists than my hometown. It, too, cropped up around one main street, but all the Stratwood shops were a heck of a lot different. Outlet stores and boutiques as far as the eye could see. Stratwood had one main street 'cause there weren't enough businesses to fill up any others. Silverton looked like it was designed that way so out-of-towners could get stuck at a traffic light, maybe see something they like, and decide to pop in and spend some money.

Mrs. Romano's Jeep stopped at a red light, and I inventoried all the fancy glass window fronts. *Flytraps*, I thought, *to lure in tourists and hold them captive until their pocketbooks are empty.* Then my eyes rested on one glass-windowed shop in particular. I saw Michael stiffen in the seat in front of me. National Insurance had a closed sign hanging in its window. I could only hope it was closed due to the fact that it was Sunday, and not for any other reason.

Finally, the stoplight released us, and we took a left turn. A few blocks down we arrived at the home of the Silverton Romanos. Michael's mom parked in front of a small Victorian-looking house. It was tall and narrow, and it had lacy shutters and a white picket fence.

As soon as Michael's mom stepped out of the Jeep, Michael turned around in his seat and smiled. "One thing," he whispered. "When you meet Giovanna, think 'wiener dog.'"

"Huh?" I said as I stepped out of the Jeep. But by then Michael's mom was ushering me through the gate and up the steps, face-to-face with Michael's cousin — Giovanna herself.

I hate to liken people to dogs, but Michael's comparison was spot-on. If Giovanna walked on four legs, she'd most definitely be a dachshund puppy. She had short, stylish dark hair and a long nose. And even though she wasn't very tall, she was somehow long-bodied, and muscular, too.

Giovanna's parents were too busy kissing Michael's mom on the cheek and making merry to pay me much attention. Giovanna, on the other hand, got right close to my face. Still thinking about what Michael said (the part about her being like a wiener dog), I thought for one terrifying moment she might stick out her tongue and lick my cheek or something. Thankfully, though, she just studied me real hard and probably counted all my clogged pores.

Michael broke in between us. "Hey, Giovanna, this is Bernie. She's majorly interested in learning some cheer moves."

Giovanna threw her arms up in the air, and I let out my breath. Just like that, I was Alice through the looking glass, and Michael and I were sitting on a red leather couch in her living room watching the choreography from last year's state championship performance, the one that took them to nationals.

The couch was just about the only piece of furniture in the entire room. I guessed the reason for that was to leave plenty of space for dancing and cheering about. There weren't a whole lot of decorations, either; however, one shelf above the fireplace housed a mishmashed collection of cheer trophies and religious statues. Porcelain members of the Holy Family (enough to make Mimi jealous) surrounded by cheap brass figurines holding pom-poms. It was like they were all cheering, "Go Baby Jesus," or something.

While the adults sat in the kitchen chatting, drinking coffee, and eating cream-filled pastry shells, Michael and I continued watching Giovanna's third-place-in-the-nation-worthy routine. And as soon as she finished it once, she started in all over again. "Did you see that, Bernie? How I got my leg so high up in the air? Watch closely this time. I'll show you again."

And she did. She was almost cartoonish in the way she tore around the room. Besides looking like a wiener dog, Giovanna also shared the pup's uncontrollable urge to yap, boundless energy, and . . . really bad breath.

I scrunched up my face and stared over at Michael. Here, far away from Mr. Stein, I finally felt safe enough to discontinue my freeze on him, and I wasn't about to let Giovanna's outstanding display of team spirit go on. There was no way to know what was being said in the kitchen with all her yelping. We'd probably already missed what we came to hear, and my ears were hurting from all the other noise I had no desire to listen to.

Michael caught my glare at last, and his eyebrows waggled a little. Obviously, he didn't know what to make of my finally paying him some attention. But he caught on quickly and turned back to his cousin. "Hey, Giovanna. Cut it for a sec, will ya?" he yelled.

"What?" she barked. "Okay. *Rude!* I could have hurt myself stopping midsplit like that, and summer camp starts next week," she huffed.

"Sorry, Giovanna. It's just, well . . . Bernie and I really enjoyed looking through those papers you sent, and we saw that story about Isabella Freemont. But you probably don't know anything about her, anyway. So where were you?" Michael drummed his fingers on his flagpole of a leg. "Oh yeah, 'Go Silverton Stallions,' right?"

"I know everything that happens in Silverton," Giovanna scoffed. I guess Michael knew just how to insult her — which came as no surprise. He knew how to insult just about everybody. Luckily, the only thing Giovanna seemed to love as much as herself (and, of course, cheerleading), was town gossip. Breathing heavily and sweating a bit, she plopped down on the couch, carving out a space between Michael and me. "Ask anything," she said. "What do you want to know?"

"Do you think someone killed her?" I asked. I wasn't gonna waste any more time getting to the point.

"Nah." Giovanna studied her chipped purple nail polish. "If you ask me, she died of a broken heart."

"What about the fire?" Michael said.

"The fire didn't kill her; everyone knows that." Giovanna rolled her eyes. "Dad thinks it was started by some kid pulling a prank. Probably a dare. I'm sure once school starts up again, some wannabe thug will start bragging about lighting the crazy old maid's house on fire and get himself arrested for arson."

"You said she had a broken heart," I reminded Giovanna.

"Yes." Giovanna made her eyelids go heavy so as to match the gravity of the matter.

"But you also said she was an old maid."

"Uh-huh."

"So who broke her heart?"

Giovanna sighed like it was me who wasn't making any sense. "*Lots* of men chased after her." She leaned in close to my face again. "I don't see *why*. I mean, she was *okay* for her age. But she did have crow's-feet, and limp hair, and . . . oh yeah, she wore really cheap clothes." Giovanna looked down at my outfit — an old powder-blue sundress Mimi had picked up at the secondhand store — and cleared her throat.

I sunk back as far away on the couch as I could get from Giovanna. "Okay, and?" I said.

"Anyway, she never seemed to show much interest in any of them. Never got married. Then, a few months ago, a rumor started going 'round town that she was engaged. I saw the ring on her finger myself. Can't believe she would've said yes to a tiny rock like that."

"So you don't know who she was planning to marry?" Michael asked.

Giovanna turned her body toward him. "Nope." She exaggerated the *p* sound so that a puff of air blew right in Michael's face.

"What's that, Giovanna?" Michael said, leaning back now, too. "I thought you knew everything." It was no small wonder Giovanna detested him . . . and he, her.

They both made unpleasant faces, and Michael said, "Want some gum, Giovanna? I really think you should have some."

Missing Michael's hint, but taking a piece anyway, Giovanna chomped while she talked. "Nobody did, but it didn't last long. I saw Isabella a few weeks before she died. Her finger was bare and her heart was broken in pieces for sure." Giovanna cupped both hands over her own heart. "You can just tell those sorts of things, ya know?"

I nodded my head in agreement. I thought I could, but I had my doubts about Giovanna's sensitivities.

"Plus, people were jealous of Isabella. They said all kinds of nasty things after the breakup."

"Like she had limp hair and wore cheap clothes?" Michael offered.

Giovanna looked like her canine instincts were kicking in and she was ready to snap, but she just ignored Michael and continued. "I have all sorts of experience with people getting jealous. You'll have to learn that, too, if you make the cheer squad, Bernie." Giovanna dropped a hand from her heart and placed it on my hand.

"Why were people jealous? What did they say?" I asked. Keeping Giovanna on track was as difficult as getting her to stop bounding around the room.

"Oh, I don't know. I guess because she lived in that big house and carved stone all day, and because *some* people thought she was pretty, they envied her. But she never gave them the time of day. And, even though nobody knew who her fiancé was, it was like he suddenly disappeared — ring and all. Then people started saying she was crazy. That either she'd made him up or she'd done him in."

I'd iced up inside and my mouth seemed frozen, too, but not Michael's. "Did you say Isabella carved stone?" He asked what I'd meant to, and he leaned backed in to hear Giovanna's answer. Guessing the gum had done the trick, I leaned in closer, as well.

"I just told you everyone thought she might've killed her fiancé, and you're worried about her sculptures?"

Michael and I both nodded.

"Did she carve portraits?" I asked, my tongue melted at last.

Giovanna looked back and forth between Michael's begging face and my own, waiting breathlessly for her reply.

"Um, no. I don't think so. I've only ever seen the one at the Silverton Art Gallery. The rest are probably gone. I bet they burned up with everything else in the fire."

Michael stood up. "You mean there's one of her carvings here in Silverton?"

"Yep."

I stood up now, too. "Can you take us to it?"

Giovanna grinned. Cheer moves. Information. It didn't seem to matter what it was, I think she liked having something we wanted. "Of course I can," she said proudly.

CHAPTER
THIRTEEN

GIOVANNA CALLED OUT, "WE'RE HEADED INTO TOWN," AS Michael and I hurried out the front door and clambered over each other, competing for the backseat of her beat-up yellow Volkswagen. In the end, it didn't matter, though. We both sat in back and Giovanna didn't seem to notice that neither of us wanted to ride shotgun.

Giovanna drove just like she cheered — loud and all over the place. She couldn't seem to get the old stick shift into gear, and it made angry, deep-down-in-the-gut noises as she turned wide corners and crossed yellow lines. I really had to wonder how Giovanna got away with this type of driving. Did all the cops look the other way just 'cause her daddy was sheriff?

At long last (really just a few minutes later, but it seemed like forever), we clunked and banged to a stop outside an old red barn on the far end of Main Street. "Ms. Greene owns the gallery," Giovanna said. "She was one of Isabella's only friends, *and* she's a former Silverton Stallions cheer captain." She said that last part like it was the most important. I pictured in my mind an older version of Giovanna, and I cringed.

We emptied the car and looked around. The words *Art*

Gallery were painted across the top in big white letters, and Giovanna's car was the only one parked in the dirt lot.

"Do you know why barns are painted red?" Michael asked. Still feeling the effects of Giovanna's driving, it was all I could do not to slip and stumble on the gravelly ground, let alone answer Michael's stupid question.

But Michael never let being ignored stop him from saying what was on his mind. "In the old days, farmers used animal blood for paint. So all the blood from the slaughterhouse wound up on the barn walls. Today they just use the regular stuff like everybody else, but they decided to stick with the red part."

"Gross," Giovanna said.

Thanks to Michael, besides having wobbly legs, my stomach started feeling all swirly-whirly, too. I felt a rush of aggravation toward him, but strange as it sounds, being annoyed with Michael just reminded me how much I'd missed having him around. The trip, Giovanna, all her enthusiastic cheer moves, and her crazy driving had distracted me from it before. However, walking alongside the red barn, careful not to bump into the sticky siding (it seemed like plain old red paint, but you never know), I felt the dread once again welling up inside me.

A string of bells on the door jingled as we entered, and Ms. Greene appeared from behind a row of vivid green and rich-purple clay pots. She wasn't nearly as old as I had been expecting — maybe in her late twenties. She wore a cherry-colored shawl around her shoulders and a glass bead dangled from a thin silver chain around her neck.

Ms. Greene said hello, and after asking Giovanna about the upcoming cheer camp, she reached out long, thin fingers to shake my hand. She moved slow and careful-like, and her breath smelled like peppermint candy. She didn't remind me of Giovanna at all — or any kind of dog for that matter. It was a pleasant surprise.

"What brings you here today?" Ms. Greene asked, looking straight at me.

Giovanna didn't give me the chance to answer for myself. "Her name's Bernie. She's my cousin Michael's friend, and they want to see Isabella Freemont's sculpture."

"Giovanna, part of being a good team captain is listening, too," Ms. Greene said. "Not just talking." Giovanna's face dropped, and Michael's lifted in a smile. I could tell he was pleasantly surprised by the gallery owner, as well.

"Now, Bernie, do you consider yourself a serious buyer? I have to warn you, Isabella's artwork is not for sale." Ms. Greene gazed at me with intense hazel-colored eyes, and then, like her handshake, came a soft and slow smile. She may have been toying with me, but if there's anything I'm good at, it's recognizing lines of grief etched on a person's face. The mention of Isabella's name had stung, and the effects of it were pricking the corners of her eyes.

Ms. Greene motioned for us to follow as she turned and walked away. I tucked my arms close to my sides. Other than the clay pots, there were glass shelves full of fragile-looking figurines and colorful paintings on the wall. None of it looked inexpensive. And all of it would make my sketches back home, even the one of Mama and me done the by the artist at the county fair, seem like beggars at a royal ball.

Ms. Greene brought us to the back of the shop and up an old wooden staircase. The boards were shiny and looked like they'd been refinished, but they still dipped and groaned as we climbed to the top. Up above, a hayloft had been turned into a cozy work space with a big, fancy table in the center of the room. On it sat a sculpture about the size of a human head. A hole had been carved in the center, and a twisty column flowed like water from one edge of the abyss to the other. It wasn't at all what I'd expected, but I knew it was Isabella's.

"What is it?" I asked.

Michael stood rigid as a lamppost, and even Giovanna was quiet and still, waiting for Ms. Greene's reply.

Ms. Greene tapped the polished table with one carefully shaped fingernail.

"Yeah, what is it?" Giovanna blurted out. Her silence lasting a whole, I don't know, five seconds.

"I'm getting there." Ms. Greene frowned — making me think her feelings for Giovanna might just mirror Michael's.

"Many artists name their pieces — even those that are abstract. But Isabella was . . . superstitious. She didn't want anything, even something as harmless as a name, attached to her work . . . Never took payment. Never signed anything."

I stepped forward. I couldn't stop myself from touching the creamy-white marble sculpture. It felt smooth in a slightly different way than the stones we usually worked with. This stone hadn't been polished by a machine; rather, it had been caressed to a glossy finish. Sanded to an almost skin-like sheen by rough paper held in whose hand? Isabella's? There was no coldness — not like that which seeped inside the cracks of my fingers when I touched one of Mr. Stein's portraits. There was an aching emptiness instead.

Ms. Greene watched me closely. Curiously. But she didn't say a word. In a store full of breakables, contact with the artwork was probably strictly prohibited. I was in dangerous territory.

I brushed off her stare. Upsetting the gallery owner wasn't high on my list of concerns. I did, however, have a list of mounting questions for her, and not a single one seemed more or less important at the moment. I finally settled on, "Can you tell us more?" hoping Ms. Greene would fill in the blanks I didn't even know were there.

She took a deep breath. "Right before I opened the gallery, I approached many of the local artists to see if they wanted to put their work on display. Isabella had this house full of sculptures, all of them stunning. But she said no. She felt her sculptures were not art, but a fulfillment of what she described as an unquenchable yearning. It didn't make sense to me. I mean, look at it."

Ms. Greene gestured to the lovely sculpture I couldn't

quite let go of. "If art is to be appreciated for its beauty and its ability to provoke emotion, her work was some of the finest." Ms. Greene sighed. "At least Isabella finally relented enough to allow me this one small piece for the gallery. I'm so thankful she did, as the rest of her work perished in the fire."

Giovanna looked smug and I expected an "I told you so" out of her, but after not one, but two slaps on the wrist, I guess she'd finally decided to keep quiet.

"How'd she do it?" I asked. "Make the sculptures, I mean."

Ms. Greene made a noise that was empty, an exhaling of air that was neither cheerful nor snide. "That's the craziest part. Her tools were old and ugly, and yet she turned out sculptures that were beyond enchanting."

My body went rigid. My hand, still frozen in place on the marble — an extension of the stone itself. "What do you mean?" I whispered, hoping I'd spoken loud enough to be heard.

Whether or not I had, Ms. Greene continued. "She used this rusty iron hammer and chisel that had been passed down through generations of her family. Apparently one of her ancestors was a blacksmith in the late 1600s."

"The dust of bones was used to harden the iron," I said, remembering what Mr. Stein had told me. I thought he was just trying to scare me, but it had been true.

All eyes landed on me — Michael's, a little forcefully. Had I forgotten to share this small detail with him? I shrugged. "History book."

Ms. Greene let out a quizzical, "Yes," and then continued. "The rest of the story is rather chilling. Maybe I shouldn't tell it."

"Please," I pleaded, and at last dropped my hand from the sculpture.

"Well . . . The tools Isabella used had a particularly grisly origin. Her ancestor, the blacksmith, was an orphan. He was taken on as an apprentice by the village smithy after his parents and sisters were robbed and then brutally murdered. After the boy returned from the fields to find the" — Ms. Greene stopped, cleared her throat, and then continued — "lifeless bodies of his family members, he was plagued by nightmares. Isabella said he had an artistic streak as well and that he sketched horrific charcoal drawings thereafter."

I gulped. The only muscle working in all of my body appeared to be my throat. I had seen the drawings on the cobblestone wall. And the blacksmith who'd taken the boy in. I'd seen it all in my nightmares. That this evil had risen from somewhere far in the past made it that much scarier. I glanced at Michael, who was focused intently now on what Ms. Greene was saying. I grimaced. What had I gotten him into?

"It gets worse," Ms. Greene said. "The blacksmith, the one who taught Isabella's ancestor his trade, took a liking to his young apprentice. He dug up the graves of the boy's parents and those of his two younger sisters. He ground their bones, and after forging the iron hammer and chisel, he baked them in the bones' dust. Then he presented the tools to his young apprentice and told him to create not what was, but what could be."

"What could be." The words rang from my lips in a faint echo of Ms. Greene.

She nodded. "The master blacksmith was later burned at the stake. As were many blacksmiths in those days — suspects of wizardry and witchcraft. Perhaps in his case it was justifiable . . . Anyway, a short while later a man's corpse was found in the same field the boy had been plowing when his family was murdered. A locket that had belonged to the boy's mother was found in the dead man's coat pocket."

"It was the boy. The young apprentice and . . . his tools," I said. "He used them to seek revenge."

"So Isabella thought," replied Ms. Greene. "The thief was a young man, and yet, he seemed to have died of natural causes. There wasn't a mark on him anywhere, or so the story goes."

A heart that simply stopped beating — like Sam's and Mrs. Finley's, and what the coroner would probably discover about Mrs. Evans's heart, too — wouldn't leave a mark, either. "But you said the master apprentice said to create what could be. That could mean someone's death, couldn't it?" I glanced fearfully again at Michael.

Ms. Greene's smile waned. "You sound like her. Isabella was convinced the hammer and chisel held some sort of power of their own . . . that one could somehow craft the future with them . . . as if such things are possible."

"Then *why* would she use them?" I asked. "Why didn't she

just get rid of the tools, destroy them if she thought they were evil or powerful or whatever?"

Ms. Greene looked at the ceiling, like somewhere up there was a jumble of words she could pull down and string together. Finally she returned her gaze to me. "Do you remember me saying the tools were passed down through multiple generations?"

I nodded.

"Isabella thought the tools had been both a blessing and curse for her family. In fact, she believed they helped her own father to amass great wealth, but they also drove him to be a selfish and ruthless man. And those who opposed him, like the thief, were met with untimely, yet seemingly natural deaths."

"But *you* don't believe the tools had *anything* to do with it?" Michael prodded.

This time I made sure Michael caught my eye, and then I gave him a small smile and a slight nod; my way of thanking him for chiming in. Giovanna, on the other hand, was staying silent even though her mouth was hanging open like she was waiting to catch a bone.

"What I'm getting at is this: I don't believe luck — good or bad — can be generated or sculpted with a chisel, or with anything else, for that matter. But Isabella believed it could. That's why she never sculpted anything but the abstract. She was afraid — afraid to end up like her father, and afraid of not having the tools if she needed them. And although the tools were

somehow at the center of her fear, she couldn't let them go."
Ms. Greene paused and then continued. "Sometimes the
things we fear losing the most begin to own us. Isabella used
the tools because she couldn't *not* use them."

"Wow." Giovanna had finally closed her mouth, only to
open it again.

Michael started to say something, too, but this time I cut
him off.

"A big house like that and all those fancy possessions . . .
Isabella Freemont probably had it all insured. Right? You know
in case of, like, the fire that actually did happen?" I said it
casually as though the thought had just occurred to me, when
really, it'd been forming in my brain since Ms. Greene started
talking.

Ms. Greene's eyes opened wide and then she closed them
for a second, like her nerves were getting raw, but she answered
me anyway. "Yes. Certainly. I referred her to the same person
who insures all the art here in the gallery."

"Who's that?" I said. "If you don't mind me asking."

"Just a local insurance agent," Ms. Greene said dismis-
sively. "Abbot Stein. His shop's right down the street if you
care to ask him more about her work. Actually," Ms. Greene
paused and shook her head. "No, I wouldn't recommend it."

"Why?" Giovanna blurted out, and for once, I was thankful for her candor.

"It doesn't matter." Ms. Greene looked years older than she
had when we first walked in the door. Her slow movements,

what I had taken for grace and poise, now just made her seem very, very tired. As she inched toward the staircase and none of us moved to follow, she finally relented. "Look, the three of you are nice enough, and if anyone could make him talk . . . I just don't think he'd take well to you pestering him, that's all. Abbot is harmless, but . . ."

"*What?*" the three of us said in unison.

"He's reclusive. Withdrawn. The only person he ever seemed very fond of was Isabella. And now she's gone . . . Come to think of it, I haven't seen him at all since Isabella's memorial service. It's probably best not to bother him."

I would've pushed further, but I could tell we'd far outworn our welcome. "Okay. Thank you," I said sincerely, and then reached out to touch Isabella's sculpture one last time.

Ms. Greene softened. She'd almost regained the shimmer of her former elegance; however, she lost it again as she fell all over herself bustling us out the door.

CHAPTER
FOURTEEN

"Isabella was crazier than I thought," Giovanna said as soon as we were back in her Volkswagen. "Should we go see that insurance agent now?"

"*No*," Michael and I said together.

"Suit yourself," Giovanna said, and then proceeded to yap all the way back to her house. She went on and on about Isabella and the tools (I could only imagine what kinda fuel we'd given her gossip train to track all over town with). Didn't matter that Michael and I weren't talking — without Ms. Greene to shut her up, there was no end to what she had to say. Not that I heard any of it, really. And feeling as blown away and flabbergasted as I was, I even ignored her crazy driving.

Then, as soon as we arrived at Giovanna's house, it was time to leave again. What had started out as a nice break from the horror back home now felt like the spin cycle on the washing machine. I was chucked back and forth between Rocco, Celeste, and Giovanna, saying my good-byes and trying to pretend the scary story I'd just heard was exactly that — a story — and not real terror leaching into my life.

Once we were back on the road, Mrs. Romano's eyes flicked to mine in the rearview mirror. "Bernie, are you feeling okay?" *No.* I certainly wasn't (and I must've looked as horrible as I felt for Mrs. Romano to ask), but it wasn't the time to spill my guts with her driving sixty-five miles per hour down a winding road. I did want to make it back home alive.

When I didn't answer, Michael released an unnatural-sounding chuckle. "I think Giovanna overwhelmed her."

I forced the corners of my lips a tiny bit upward. That seemed to satisfy Mrs. Romano, and the car ride home passed in another silent blur. By the time we reached my house, it was evening and the sky was torn in two. It seemed to be deciding between daylight and darkness, and darkness was winning.

Michael gave me a pained look as I slowly slipped out of the back of the SUV. I'm sure he felt awful about letting me go inside my house alone with Mr. Stein and the tools just a football's throw from my window. And he had to be stumped as to why I'd avoided him from the day Mrs. Evans died until we were sitting on Giovanna's couch in Silverton. Little did he know, I wasn't done ignoring him yet.

But I simply pushed up the corners of my lips again and waved good-bye. I still couldn't bring myself to tell Michael about his portrait (especially with his mother around), and there wasn't anything more he could do. I slammed the door shut, and Michael's mom pulled the Jeep away. The taillights grew smaller and smaller in the distance and then finally disappeared around the corner. With me just standing there watching, the two red dots took my best ally with them.

Home was supposed to feel safe, a sanctuary from the

outside world. But Mr. Stein had turned my house into the furthest thing from it. Every square inch of my skin stood on alert as I walked in through the front door.

It was Mimi's bingo night, and she was over at the town hall. Dad appeared, grunted a hello, and then disappeared to some out-of-the-way corner of the house. Not exactly a warm welcome, but much better than being greeted with heartbroken tears and news of another victim.

My steps felt only slightly lighter as I made my way into the kitchen. Dishes were piled in the sink and trays sat on the counter, signs that Mama and Mr. Stein had already eaten. Good. I really wasn't up to trudging out to the carriage house just then.

I wasn't hungry, either. However, I went through the motions of toasting a bagel, anyway — trying to cling to something normal. I spread cream cheese on the bagel. Then I drizzled honey and sprinkled crunchy granola over the top. I set my food on the table and took a seat looking out the kitchen window.

The carriage house was just out of sight from where I was sitting, but the headstones in the backyard, those I could see. As I stared out at the markers lit by moonlight, I didn't know what I wanted to do most: scream, cry, or punch something really hard. Whatever I was expecting from our trip to Silverton, I hadn't quite been prepared for what I'd found out.

Yet, when I started to peel back the layers of scary, frightful things I'd learned, I found that at the bottom of it all, I had a budding idea of how to stop Mr. Stein. That idea warmed my heart and gave me hope — hope that I could keep Mr. Stein from chiseling anyone else out of existence, hope that I really could save Michael.

Without the tools, I didn't think Mr. Stein would be as big of a menace. If I were to take them from him, anything was possible . . . I pushed the thought away as quickly as it came. It's difficult to keep a candle of hope lit inside when everything around you is so very grim.

I was sitting there, sorting through thoughts too big for my brain, when a tall, thin shadow crossed one of the headstones outside. There was only one person I knew who would be slinking around our backyard at this time of night, casting such a bristly looking shadow.

I'm not gonna lie and pretend I wasn't afraid — that I leaped up from my chair, feeling brave and vengeful. The truth is, my fear darn near stopped me. It would have, if my want hadn't been stronger. No matter how terrified I felt, I wanted more than anything to stop Mr. Stein before he took another life.

I left my bagel untouched and stood slowly from the table. If I went out the back door, Mr. Stein would see me for sure, so instead, I slipped into a jacket hanging on a hook by the front door and headed out that way. Stupid, careless, and trembling with fear, I followed Mr. Stein and his cursed tools outside.

The street looked empty. Most of the houses were lit from

television sets and reading lamps, but the large lots with all those sheds and garages were dark, perfect places for Mr. Stein to cover himself with the cloak of night.

I clutched my light jacket to my chest and looked for any signs of movement. There were none. I was about to head back inside to my bagel when I caught sight of a shadow shrinking in the streetlight on the far end of the block. Someone had just turned the corner. The same corner Michael had turned not long before in his mother's SUV.

As had happened so many times since Mr. Stein entered my life, I felt the cold, breath-stealing grasp of terror wash over me. Not now! I wasn't ready for him to go after Michael. I would never be ready. I didn't know whether to run back to the carriage house and search for a new portrait of my friend with his wide fingers and skinny wrists (no, I couldn't face that) . . . or to chase Mr. Stein down.

Making a split-second decision, I crept forward, moving low and as quickly as I could. I tried to stay out of the path of streetlights. Overgrown ivy on the sidewalk threatened to make me stumble and trip. I took my steps carefully, and all the while I hoped like mad Mr. Stein wouldn't glance back and see me. It wasn't long before there were but a few yards between me and Abbot Stein.

I held back, just an instant, and my urge to trail him began to fade. What could I possibly do to stop this? I couldn't bear to find Michael the way I'd found Mrs. Evans. I'd . . .

I'd ... I'd end up like Mama, cowering away, lost forever between the walls of my room.

Just then a dog howled at me from behind a fence. I scrambled behind a thick and thorny bush, holding my breath as Mr. Stein turned an ear toward the sound. As on the day Michael and I spied on him in the carriage house, Mr. Stein's eyes were completely sheeted in white.

I shrank deeper into the bush. A thorn poked a hole in my shirt and tore into the skin on my lower back. I held my breath. It seemed like I had lived a lifetime before Mr. Stein swiveled his head back around and continued on his path. He didn't appear to be having any trouble maneuvering through the dark with his milky-coated eyes. He must've been moving on something other than eyesight entirely.

I wondered if I should try jumping him. As wiry as he was, I thought I might just stand a chance if I caught him unaware. But he might be stronger than he looked, especially if he really was some sort of gateway to evil, the way his eyes made him appear.

As I was searching for the perfect angle from which to flail my assault, Mr. Stein took an unexpected turn and headed in the opposite direction of Michael's home. The dread that had been churning violent circles in my stomach lessened, but did not disappear entirely. He was not trailing the green SUV after all. Or if he was, he was taking a detour, 'cause he was headed straight for the cemetery.

The smartest thing to do would've been to let him go and just pray that he never stood outside my own door, bone-dusted iron tools in hand. At this late hour, it was unlikely that there would be any *living* person in the cemetery for Mr. Stein or his tools to harm. That was, except for me, of course, if I dared to follow.

I watched Mr. Stein cross the street and enter through the stone pillars on the south end. There was no gate to open. No hinges to be sprung. It wasn't at all like the cemetery fences you hear about in ghost stories with wrought-iron poles that shimmy and whine in the wind. I always thought those stories were silly, trying to make it seem like the purpose of a gate was to keep ghostly things in, or daring children out. Like a creaky, old gate would stop either one.

But it was never truly the gates that were meant to hold people back — it was the fear, and again, I couldn't let that stop me. Knowing what I knew (about the tools) and what I didn't know (how long before Mr. Stein would use them to take Michael's, or someone else's life), I couldn't risk not following.

I retreated slightly, but only so I could backtrack and cut up Thirty-Second Street and sneak around to the other entrance. I was pretty sure the northern entrance was the one Michael had used when he'd snuck up on me. I only hoped I would have as much luck slipping in undetected.

As I ran, the portrait in my pack slammed over and over into my side. It wasn't something I thought about anymore. I just always had it with me. By the time I reached the entrance on the opposite end, I was out of breath and my heart was putting forth its best effort to escape my rib cage. Using one of the stone pillars to lean against, I gulped in the crisp night air.

When my breathing returned to normal, I walked into the cemetery only to find it not nearly as charming as it was in the sunlight. My friends, the trees, had turned on me. They reached their scraggly arms in all directions, pointing me down dark and shadowy paths. I didn't trust them to keep me hidden. Seemed like any minute they would twist away their branches and betray my presence to Mr. Stein.

As I stumbled through the darkness, I noticed a quiet, grating noise in the background. It had the tone of metal on stone, but in my mind, I saw fingernails scraping coffin lids. I scanned the shadows, trying to see where the noise was coming from and realized — I was lost.

It was all I could do to swallow a scream. I knew my way perfectly well in the daytime, but at night everything looked different. And that scraping noise? It was getting louder and louder, and I had no idea where it was coming from.

Then a mouse crossed my path, harmless, small, and gray, but it was enough to finally send my fear spiraling out of control. So I ran. Forgot about being brave. I just spun around and dug my toes into the grass, giving up all intention of locating Mr. Stein in the graveyard.

On a day where I hadn't just learned of the eerie powers of iron hardened by the dust of human bones, I'd like to think I would've been daring enough to stay. Who knows, I might have even gone back in, once I'd calmed myself, if I hadn't tripped. The corner of my shoe caught on a patch of grass that wasn't neatly manicured — not yet, anyway — just a piece of sod resting slightly higher than the rest. And, as I picked myself up, I saw the familiar portrait of Sam Fuller. He was smiling down on me from his newly placed headstone.

Now maybe, just maybe, it was Sam or Isabella helping me along, causing me to trip like that. 'Cause, instead of letting out the scream that had been building inside me, a light flicked on in my head. Sam Fuller's freshly dug grave took the idea that was budding earlier and gave it wings. A grave! That's just what I needed to get rid of the tools. And I just so happened to know when one would be available. It certainly wasn't the most saintly idea I'd ever had, but something told me it would take an action less than saintly to stop this business once and for all.

This time, I couldn't hold back my hope. It soared.

CHAPTER
FIFTEEN

THE HARDEST PART OF MY PLAN WAS WAITING UNTIL Thursday to carry it out. And Thursday was the wrong, wrong, wrongest day. The day that tethered my hopes and dragged them back down. Thursday was the day I didn't want to think about, the day the Morrison family dreaded most, and the day I wanted to X off my calendar all together. But Thursday was the only day it could be.

Michael showed up first thing Monday morning, probably thinking we'd brainstorm ideas together after what we'd learned in Silverton. However, the previous night had been too close of a call. Even if Mr. Stein hadn't been following his mother's Jeep down the street, he very well could've been. Until I carried my plan through on Thursday (assuming we were all still alive and breathing by then), Michael Romano was officially out of my life. And I wasn't gonna risk backing down to his moping face, either. I sent Mimi to the door to turn him away.

She was frowning when she came back, and while she unloaded a strawberry scone onto my plate. Then she sighed heavily and left the room. She wasn't happy with my decision to keep turning Michael away, and even less pleased that I wouldn't tell her why.

I think Mimi wanted me to feel lonely and to dwell on how empty the kitchen felt as I ate my breakfast without him. If that was truly the case, she wouldn't have been disappointed.

I tried to switch my focus to my plan. I needed a box . . . and some soup . . . but other than that, I hadn't a clue. Some plans are complicated. Some plans keep you busy right up until the big event so you won't have time to think of all the things that can go wrong. Big events, like weddings and funerals. My idea wasn't one of those. It required very little real planning — leaving all sorts of time wide open for worrying and second guessing . . . and missing my friend.

There was also the matter of me wondering if I might scratch part of the plan and just keep the tools for myself. Sure, I knew it was wrong, but I thought maybe, just maybe, if Isabella had been able to, I could hold on to them, as well. I could get the tools away from Mr. Stein and still fix my family. Ms. Greene had said Isabella's ancestor had been told to chisel "what could be," right? Making portraits or something else entirely — could I carve out a happier life for us all?

When I visited my mama later that day, I smiled for her and fluffed her pillow and pretended I didn't see the black circles beneath her eyes or the sonogram photo that had reappeared on her nightstand. The one that read, "Baby Boy Morrison." Mimi still hadn't told her about Mrs. Evans. Her fragile state could only take so much.

Like Mama, I holed up those next few days, worrying and fretting until Wednesday, when I finally left the house to go to the hardware store. I spent my entire summer allowance on one item, a small metal box with a flip-top lid and a combination lock. After I'd laid my money on the counter and walked out the door, I ran straight into Michael. The way he popped out as soon as I'd exited the building proved that us bumping into each other wasn't a coincidence. He'd been watching me.

"Now how are you going to afford that cheerleading uniform?" he joked.

The first thing I did was scan the area for Mr. Stein, and then I looked directly at Michael and said, "What are you doing here?" It was hard to sound too angry, considering I'd woken up that very morning just praying he was still alive, praying that Mr. Stein wouldn't etch Michael right out of existence before I had the chance to stop him.

I dragged Michael around the corner. Now that we were alone and face-to-face, I thought about coming clean about his portrait. But I knew Michael well enough to know there wasn't a snowball's chance of him staying out of it if I did. He'd just wind up dead.

So I reminded myself this was for his own good, and then I took in a deep breath and did my best to snarl. "You think Giovanna acts like a dog, do you? Well, it must run in the family. You're a lost puppy chasing me everywhere, and I'm sick of it." I pushed my finger into his chest. "I don't need your help. *So stop following me!*"

Michael seemed to be searching my face, looking for an

answer. "Why are you doing this, Bernie? What are not telling me?"

"I needed you to take me to Silverton, but I don't need you anymore. You're always pushing in where you don't belong. And if you don't leave me alone and someone else dies . . ." I paused as I felt a tremble running through my body at the thought that it could be him. "It's going to be your fault."

My finger was still on his chest, and I felt his ribs heave with an intake of air. "Okay," he said quietly, and exhaled. "I'll leave you alone."

I dropped my hand, and then, not able to bear the look of hurt on his face, I walked away and didn't look back.

It didn't take long to find the perfect bush just inside the southern entrance of the graveyard. It was thick with dark leaves. My hands were still shaking as I reached all the way through to the muddy soil below. I couldn't stop thinking about Michael. If only I could make it this far the next night, we'd be home free (or so I thought), and then I could apologize. I ditched the box, making sure it wasn't visible from above.

Once I was back at the house, I made a beeline for the den. I wasn't stupid enough to try calling the funeral home from there, but I did need to grab the number from the Rolodex on Mimi's desk.

I flew into the room, still upset and raw from my confrontation with Michael. Dad lifted his head, and Mr. Stein took a step back, knocking Mimi's silver-plated crucifix off the wall behind him. He bent down to pick it up, keeping his eyes, the same slick color as Mimi's cross, locked on me.

Dad cleared his throat, perhaps to hide a rare laugh that seemed to escape with Mr. Stein's mishap. Then he said, "This is fine work, Abbot. Fine work." He was appraising a portrait in his hands — it looked like a duplicate of the one Mr. Stein had etched for Mrs. Evans; it must've been made after I'd destroyed the first.

Mr. Stein stood up and slipped a wire over a nail on the wall to rehang the cross. Then, with a face made of angles and dark shadows (Mimi's cooking had somehow failed to fatten him up), he said, "You're looking well, Bernie. You're even feistier than I thought."

It was a strange thing for Mr. Stein to say, but, then again, everything about Mr. Stein was strange. Maybe he'd thought I wouldn't be able to look him in the eye after what had happened to Mrs. Evans. If he thought I would quake and tremble in his presence this time, he was wrong.

I ignored his comment and snatched the entire Rolodex off Mimi's desktop. Perhaps I was too brazen, reaching right in front of him with a steady arm and a slight smirk on my face, or perhaps a little too sure of myself as I turned on my heels and walked out of the room. If I'd realized the tone of his words meant something, would things have gone differently the following evening? Maybe. But most likely not. I didn't know it then, but my plan was doomed before it ever started.

CHAPTER
SIXTEEN

WHEN THURSDAY MORNING FINALLY SLID INTO PLACE AS IT always does, following Wednesday and before Friday, it wasn't necessary to fake being sick. Not like I'd planned. I hadn't slept well since who knows when, due to my nightmares and all the worrying I'd done waiting for this day to come. And it showed. I was a right fright when I slunk down to the kitchen with a long face and big, heavy bags under my eyes. I hardly touched my breakfast, and Mimi sent me straight back to bed, which was a good thing, since my stomach was churning like a cement mixer again.

I spent most of the day staring at Isabella's portrait — looking at her frozen gray face — and feeling guilty about Michael. I slid my finger over the smooth rock like it was a good-luck charm . . . or a maybe a worry stone. But it did nothing to soothe my fraying nerves. Nor did thinking about Mama and Thomas or about what an awful day this was to be attempting my plan.

Mimi knocked on my door around lunchtime. I dropped Isabella's portrait on the carpet beside my bed and slid beneath the covers as she carried in a tray with apple slices and a peanut butter, banana, and honey sandwich.

"I wish I didn't have to leave you alone tonight." Mimi set the tray on the nightstand beside me. "I know how much Mrs. Evans liked you. She would've wanted you there . . ." Mimi said, her thoughts trailing off at the end.

That didn't sit well on the pile of bad feelings in my stomach. There definitely wasn't any room left for food. I pushed the tray aside. "Mimi, will you make me some soup for dinner tonight?" I said. "I'm starting to feel better, and I think I might be hungry by then."

"Of course, Bernie."

"And don't worry about Mama and Mr. Stein. I'm sure I'll be up to bringing them soup later, as well," I added.

Mimi bit her bottom lip, "Oh dear, your mother . . . I don't like leaving her, either."

"She'll understand," I said. "Just go and say a few extra Hail Marys for the both of us."

Mimi patted the sheet covering my legs. "You know I will, Bernie. I always do."

The thought of Mimi praying for me brought a bit of comfort and I started to sit up in bed. Mimi stopped me with her hand. "Get some more rest. I'll check on you before I leave."

"Thanks, Mimi. I'll try." I most definitely could've used some rest and peace, and some sort of supernatural ability to just bypass this awful day altogether now that it was here. But that wasn't possible, and my wanting heart was begging to get it over with. Sometimes, when you know a hard thing's coming, the waiting is even more difficult than being able to dig yourself right in.

I paced and fretted the afternoon away until I finally heard Mimi's footsteps outside my door again. Then I hopped under the covers once more before Mimi poked her head in to blow me a kiss. Feeling extra sappy, I blew one right back at her. Something I hadn't done for ages.

As soon as I heard the front door shut behind her and Dad, I packed Isabella's portrait into my backpack and slipped quietly down the stairs and into the kitchen. I left the lights off the entire way. The last thing I needed was to draw Mr. Stein's attention.

Not seeing any movement in the backyard, I scooped a bowl of beef-and-barley soup out of the pot on the stove and then turned up the heat on the burner. I was still too nervous to eat, but I wanted to bring some up to Mama before . . . well, before I did anything else.

Mama's room was still and silent when I pushed open the door. The shades were drawn back, but with the sun already starting to set, the room was fuzzy with evening light.

"Mama?" I called out softly.

"I'm awake." Mama's voice cracked from somewhere under the covers.

"Mama, can I see you?"

My mother slid up to a sitting position from under the lightweight summer comforter. Her white-blond hair was matted against her head, and her eyes were puffy and rimmed in red — the only color visible, what with her face as white as her ivory nightgown.

"Today's the day . . ." I said.

"Yes." My mother's voice cracked again, but I knew she hadn't caught the double meaning of my words. I wouldn't have expected her to, of course. She had no way of knowing.

I probably should have said more — how I was sad, and how I missed Thomas, too. But instead, I set the bowl of soup down on her nightstand and touched the palm of my empty hand to her cheek. "Mmmm . . . Your hand's so warm, Bernie," she said. Mama smiled at me, but the smile didn't reach her eyes.

"I love you, Mama," I said.

"I love you, too." She shivered and turned to look at the open window. The temperature was beginning to drop outside. The room was still stuffy, but the draft was cold. I walked over to close the window for her, pausing a minute to look down on the carriage house below. Little rays of light were trying to escape through the cracks of Mr. Stein's door.

"I think I'll try to sleep now," Mama said.

I returned to her side thinking she'd lie back down, but Mama remained sitting with her head tilted down and her shoulders curled inward. Her knobby knees created peaks beneath the bedding, and they seemed to be stretching out to connect with the porcelain-like skin of her forehead.

Looking at her that way split my heart with want. Part of me wanted to fold her body further, cradle her within my arms.

Stay with her and bear some of her misery. At the very least I probably should've touched my hand to her cheek again before I left. But I couldn't. I couldn't hold her pain along with the weight of what I was about to do, and a larger part of my heart was already out the door.

As I quietly left her room, I questioned my plan one final time: *What could be?* Could I make this different? Could I un-break my mama's heart if the tools were mine? Even if I could, even if she got better, would I ever be able to stop causing her pain? I would always remind her of Thomas. I would always be me, unsaintly Bernie, no matter what kind of future I attempted to chisel out for my family.

I walked down the landing. With the door now shut between me and Mama, I felt how utterly alone I was. Every noise I could hear was made by me, and it was the rapid sound of my heart beating that was loudest in my ears. It pounded and throbbed with fear. What if I just turned around? What if, like Mama, I went to my room and hid beneath the covers until this night was over? I almost did, but then my thoughts turned to Michael, and I kept walking.

Just as I made it to the bottom of the stairs, the doorbell rang. My fear was momentarily replaced with surprise, and without Mimi around to hear it, I cursed freely and then threw open the door.

It was as though I'd magically conjured Michael here by thinking about him, and that was the last thing I wanted, or was it? I gritted my teeth. Michael stared back at me the same

way he had the day he'd brushed his fingers across mine —
tight-lipped and grimly serious. "Sorry. I know you don't want
me here, but when you didn't show up at the church with your
dad and Mimi, I got worried." His floppy hair was a mess, and
his sneakers were untied. There was a small waver in the way
he breathed in air and then let it back out. He was a nervous
wreck.

Part of me knew it would be best to find another stinging
thing to say, something that would make him want to leave,
but I wasn't myself. I was weaker and more afraid than I'd ever
been, and just the sight of him was reassuring. "Get in here," I
said before I realized what I was doing.

Michael followed me to the kitchen. I started up with the
pacing again, but it felt different with him waiting silently in
the corner. It felt better. Less lonely. I was so grateful to him
for showing up. After all the awful things I'd said, he still
cared enough about me to come back. But now that he was
here, how could I possibly keep him safe? I groaned inwardly
as another wave of fear and dread washed over me.

I glanced at Michael. In the dim light, I could only just
make out his outline across the kitchen. Yet everything about
the way he was standing — all jittery and alert to my every
move — made it clear that he was more concerned about me
than he was about himself, and that wasn't fair. He still didn't
know what was truly at stake. I stopped pacing and walked
across the kitchen to be near him.

"What?" Michael asked when I didn't say anything. He

must've sensed that I had something to tell him, but that I was having trouble spitting it out.

"Mr. Stein . . . He sort of, well, he might have his sights on you. He was etching your portrait . . . before I destroyed it."

With the lights off I couldn't see his face all that well, even standing as close as we were, but I could imagine it turning the exact shade of green as the sea-foam colored walls in my bedroom. I heard him suck in a deep breath of air. "Oh," he said. I could tell he was searching for a way to turn this bit of information into a joke, but he couldn't.

"I'm sorry," I said, and I deeply meant it. "I thought maybe if you weren't around, Mr. Stein would just forget about you."

Michael looked up at the ceiling and shook his head disbelievingly.

"What?" I said. "It's working, ain't it? You're still here, aren't you?"

Michael smirked. "I am, and you're not getting rid of me this time." He reached forward and draped his arms over my shoulders. I let him pull me toward him. It felt weirdly good, tucked close to his chest — my head fit neatly beneath his much larger one. Michael held me for a while, and my stomach, which felt like it'd been roiling for weeks, slowed to a quiet shuffle. I hadn't wanted Michael to be here, but I hadn't wanted him to be my friend in the first place, either. I'd been wrong on both counts.

"Now that that's settled, can we just hurry up and find a way to stop Mr. Stein?"

Michael came with me as I slipped through the den and out into the garage. I dropped my backpack (with Isabella's portrait inside) behind a stone waiting for its turn to be sandblasted. It kicked up a cloud of dust, and Michael and I nearly burst a lung trying to keep from choking on the swirling dust particles.

We rushed back to the kitchen with tears in our eyes. When we'd each taken a sip of water, and when I could speak again, I said, "Ready?"

Michael nodded and I filled another bowl of beef-and-barley soup. I placed it on a tray, not bothering to grab a spoon. Mr. Stein wouldn't need one. Feeling a gush of energy now that my plan was finally, *finally* being put into action, I sprang to the back door with my only weapon, soup. It was steaming, and now, so was I.

Michael stayed close on my heels as I bounded out the back door and down the paver pathway with the tray in my hands. He was right beside me as I reached the carriage house.

"Stand there," I whispered, and pointed beside the door.

Michael pasted himself against the wooden slats in a place where he wouldn't be spotted right away when Mr. Stein opened up the carriage house door. I knocked sharply, waited a few minutes, and then knocked again.

"What is it?" Mr. Stein snarled as he swung open the door. A brief, sweet sigh of relief floated through my lungs. Not that I'd ever seen him without it, but Mr. Stein was wearing his overcoat.

I lunged forward, knowing Mr. Stein would wonder why I was hanging around so long if I didn't move swiftly. Pretending to trip, I caused the beef-and-barley soup to splash out of the bowl. I aimed for Mr. Stein's face. And just like that, Michael was on him before Mr. Stein could react. He'd jumped out from behind the door as I'd hurled the soup, and was already pulling on the lapels of Mr. Stein's black overcoat.

"Ummph." Mr. Stein struggled against Michael as he shook the soup broth from his eyes and bits of carrots and barley from his face. But Michael was a step ahead. He slipped the coat from Mr. Stein's arms and took off, full sprint.

"Run, Michael!" I screamed. I stood back, watching, my tongue heavy as a rock in my mouth. How could I have put Michael in danger? It should've been me doing this part, not him. As Michael sprang for the garage, overcoat in his hands, Mr. Stein let out an angry hiss and used his hands to wipe the rest of the soup from his face. Then, without so much as a glance in my direction, he charged after Michael.

Michael was far enough ahead that the back door creaked and then swung shut between them. Mr. Stein fumbled with the handle and then finally yanked it open. Michael would have a sliver of time alone in the garage, but I wasn't quite sure it would be enough.

I waited. I heard the garage door slide open and then the sound of footsteps running down the front pavement before I made my next move.

Quickly, but quiet as a whispered prayer, I took my turn

creeping into the garage. I left the lights off again, knowing everything might be lost if they drew Mr. Stein's attention back to the house.

I reached behind the mammoth headstone. My bag was where we'd left it earlier and my heart swelled with relief as I lifted it up and felt the added weight. The tools were in the bag. Michael had done it! *God bless him.* Michael had done it! I pulled the drawstrings tight, threw the bag over my shoulder, and slipped out the back door.

Michael's next step was to head west — the opposite direction of the cemetery. Even though Michael was long and lanky, he was better at loping than sprinting. I worried his laid-back strides wouldn't keep him a step ahead of Mr. Stein for long.

If he reached the Wood Mill, five blocks away, he was to drop the overcoat in plain sight — just discard it in the middle of the sidewalk — and then head into the open space reserve. *Five blocks, just five blocks. PLEASE,* I pleaded under my breath. *PLEASE let Michael find a good place to hide there until this is over.*

I couldn't believe I'd just sent Mr. Stein chasing after Michael when I'd been desperately trying to keep them apart. But Michael had bought me more time than I ever could've hoped for on my own. Even if I'd somehow managed to shake Mr. Stein without Michael, I would've needed to double back. Now I could head straight for the cemetery, and the biggest danger Michael faced was from what I was lugging in my backpack, right?

I shuddered.

No. Mr. Stein's heart was black and twisted. Tools or no tools, there was no telling what he'd do. In that moment, I doubted every ounce of my plan, but it was too late not to see it through.

Michael and Mr. Stein had disappeared around a bend in the road by the time my feet hit the sidewalk. My thoughts chased after them, but I turned left and bolted for the graveyard.

CHAPTER
SEVENTEEN

THE NIGHT WAS THE COLOR OF SLICK, SYRUPY OIL. IT DIDN'T help that almost all the houses had darkened windows. No television sets or reading lamps lighting up friendly faces inside. The houses were most likely empty on account of Mrs. Evans's rosary service. As likeable as she was, believers and nonbelievers were sure to be turning up at the church in her honor. The church was where I wanted to be, but wasn't. And wanting wasn't getting me anywhere.

I pumped my feet up and down as fast as God made me able, trying to make up for all the other things I couldn't control. Taking the same path I'd been on Sunday night, I once again ducked in and out of shadows. This time, not having to worry about Mr. Stein looking back, I used the wide southern entrance and darted between the stone columns and into the slumbering cemetery.

Right away, I began rustling through the bush just inside the entrance. I felt all kinds of heebie-jeebies as I sunk my fingers into the pit of thorns and leaves. Luckily, no bony skeleton hands played tug-of-war with me as I lifted out the metal box. Before we'd dumped it in the bush, I'd set the combination to 7-2-3. Seven for the month of July, and twenty-three for the day Mrs. Evans died.

The box was slim and felt like a frozen dead fish in my hands as I carried it through the cemetery. I watched my feet as I weaved back and forth through the headstones. Even the grass seemed grim tonight. The thick, dark-green blades gave way beneath my size six sneakers, leaving smooshed-down footprints in the otherwise perfect sod.

When I'd called the funeral home on Wednesday night, I'd been told Mrs. Evans's grave was at plot J27. If I'd thought he could find it in the dark, I would've used myself for bait and had Michael do this part instead. However, I was much more familiar with the cemetery. I pictured its location in my head — same row as our family plot, just twelve grave sites down.

While I was faking illness and truly feeling queasy at the same time, and while Mimi was tending to me back home, and while the sun was still shining bright, a hole was being bur-rowed out for Mrs. Evans's final resting place. I knew the hole wouldn't be six feet deep, as the saying goes. I knew 'cause I asked Dad about it once when we were delivering a headstone. (These are the types of things you wonder when you're walk-ing above the dead, hoping that even with all the grass and dirt and hard coffin lids between them and your toes, the bodies are as far down as possible.)

Anyway, Dad said every state has its own laws when it comes to burying their dead. Some states dig up only two or three feet of dirt, but most go down much farther. Ours just so happens to be one of the deeper-digging states. Everybody sleeping in the Stratwood Cemetery was a solid twelve feet under.

Mrs. Evans's body would soon join them. *Twelve feet.* Deep enough I could drop down a Bible-sized metal box, swipe in a few kicks of dirt, and it would go unnoticed even when they lowered in her coffin.

Even though all the states have different laws when it comes to their cemeteries, there is one that is the same no matter where you live. Once a person is buried, they can't be dug up. Not unless the court gives its say-so. "Don't disturb the dead" and all that. So a grave was the perfect place to hide the iron hammer and chisel.

It occurred to me that dug-up bones were the start of all this, but that was hundreds of years ago. I highly doubted there were any blacksmiths robbing graves these days, especially in quiet, old Stratwood. In a way, it was a fitting end for the tools that were coated in the dust of that poor family's bones. That is: They would finally be laid to rest. The metal box I planned on placing them in would act as a coffin of sorts.

My thoughts were wandering, and I tried to shut them off. I knew by then Mr. Stein would've found the empty pockets in his overcoat. Michael may have bought me more time, but I still needed to hurry.

I found row J and started counting plots as I went so I wouldn't get lost again: J1–J3 belonged to the Schell family, J4–J6 were still empty. J7 and J8 were filled by Mr. and Mrs. Jones. J9 for Mrs. Nelson, J10–J15 belonged to none other than —

I stopped cold.

Every part of me froze, from the hairs on my head to the tips of my toenails, except for my heart — it beat wildly out of control. I was used to the pitch blackness of the night by then, and I could plainly see where, right on our family headstone, just above the plot reserved for yours truly, was the likeness of my face etched in stone.

My very own portrait of death.

My laughing eyes, my nose, and my tight-mouthed grin stared back at me. I gasped for air, but none came. My lungs were empty. My hope was crushed, chewed on, and spit out, all at once. It was over. This, my portrait, meant I'd failed. And miserably, horribly so. Mr. Stein was going to win . . . *and I was going to die*!

Thoughts flooded back into my brain with a panicky pace. I'd taken all the empty tiles . . . I'd cracked them far beyond any usability . . . Mr. Stein had then brought his tools to this wide blank target in the cemetery — my family marker . . . That scraping noise I'd heard, it was my own life ending . . . Mr. Stein hadn't expected me to be in shock when I'd bumped into him in the den; he was expecting me to be on my deathbed . . . I was so worried about Michael, I'd entirely missed the fact that Mr. Stein had turned his sights on me.

That's when I started to feel the tingle in my fingers, the even sicker feeling in my stomach and the tightening in my chest. The metal box slipped from my grasp. I flung the bag off my shoulder and onto the ground in front of me. I pulled open the drawstring and spilled the contents onto the grass.

Isabella's portrait tumbled out first. I knew it wasn't possible, but her stone-etched eyes seemed to flash with a fear mirroring my own. Next, the tools toppled out onto the grass. Shiny and silver, they winked at me between the grassy blades. Not a spot of rust on either one. I sunk to my knees on the ground that would soon be my grave.

These weren't them.

These were not the cursed hammer and chisel. These were new, and not the tools that would end my life.

I shook my head, noticing the way a lack of air was making me feel dizzy and light-headed. I struggled to keep the dark spots in my vision from connecting and turning my world entirely black. *This must be what it feels like right before your heart stops working*, I thought. *This must be what Isabella and Mrs. Evans and all the others felt before they died.*

I was so caught up in all that hopeless terror that when Mr. Stein's cackle pierced through the ringing in my ears, I didn't even jump.

"I see you've discovered my latest work of art, Bernie — the resemblance is superb, don't you think?" He talked like we were merely in Ms. Greene's gallery, admiring one of the paintings on the wall. "I am surprised, however, that you didn't find it sooner. Say, on the night you followed me here."

I fought against eyelids as heavy as two anvils and glanced

up. Mr. Stein was standing above me, blocking the path to Mrs. Evans's grave. "I waited for you, anxious to chisel in the final touches, but you disappointed me. Perhaps you're not as bold as I thought. "

Mr. Stein's jaw tightened as he waved his hand in front of it. "No matter. You're here now, aren't you? And I have your full attention."

His overcoat was still missing. Mr. Stein wore a dark, short-sleeved shirt and crisp blue jeans, and for the first time I noticed the worn, leather sheath strung from his waist. His thumb carefully caressed a sharp edge of iron extending from it. Mr. Stein followed my gaze. "Ah, yes. These." He stopped stroking the tools and gave the sheath a friendly pat. "They are what you were hoping to find in my coat, are they not? What's wrong, Bernie? Don't you like the replacements?"

I couldn't answer. I couldn't say anything. The prick in my chest was spreading to my throat, and the dots in my vision had grown into caverns.

"You're like me, Bernie." Mr. Stein glanced down at Isabella's portrait on the ground, and for a second, I thought I saw doubt flicker across his face. "And like her, too, I suppose," he said, his voice dropping to an octave so low he almost sounded sad.

"Isabella," I said, my voice strained.

"Yes, Isabella. She was beautiful, but she was stubborn like you. She was careful, too. Kept the tools locked in a glass case and wouldn't even let me hold them for a proper appraisal. All those fragile sculptures of hers, and it was a pair of rusty tools she didn't want me to touch." Mr. Stein looked down at the hammer and chisel, and again, patted them lovingly.

"Isabella was used to men pursuing her, for both her looks and her money, of course. But I was different. I saw beyond all that."

Somehow I managed a cold, disbelieving laugh.

Mr. Stein's eyes flashed with anger and then clouded with white as he tore the iron hammer and chisel from the pouch at his side. He scraped the sharp edge of the chisel across the face of my portrait and I felt incredible pain ignite on my cheek — like it was being seared with hot iron.

I yelped and Mr. Stein pulled the tool away from my stone image, and continued. "I saw that Isabella was scared and alone; lonely — like I was, and like you are. She just needed someone to help her carry the burden."

Mr. Stein's jaw was hard as ever, but the lines around his eyes and the pucker of his lips were heavy with misery. "But she refused to love anyone. She refused me."

Imagine that, I thought, but kept it to myself this time. I didn't dare to even groan.

"Then, Ms. Greene told me about Isabella's ancestor, and about the tools, and I felt sorry for Isabella. Nobody believed her, not even her friend. Nobody loved Isabella, nobody understood her the way I did . . ." The misery spread from the corners of his eyes and lips until his entire face dragged downward and even the bones in his jaw seemed to sag.

"I know what you mean," I said softly. It seemed with Mr. Stein distracted, a bit of my strength was returning. I wanted, needed to keep him talking. "The engagement ring Isabella wore — it was from you, wasn't it? Did you blackmail her, or . . ." My thoughts trailed off. I pictured Mr. Stein using the tools to etch not a headstone portrait, but a pleasant little scene . . . man and wife? A wedding portrait?

Mr. Stein sniffled and wiped his nose with the back side of his hand, and then he nodded. "She wouldn't accept my advances otherwise, so I did what I had to do. I took the tools, nothing else. I don't know why she even bothered with a police report. I didn't want her riches, I just wanted *her*. I would never misuse the tools like her father had."

"Right, 'cause using the tools to control people and for murder isn't nearly as awful as using them for money," I said, realizing that if I had the gumption for sarcasm, the strength of my portrait was indeed waning. If Mr. Stein hadn't chiseled in the final touches, maybe its dark power was incomplete. Maybe my death wasn't sealed. Then again . . .

It had been foolish of me to ridicule him. Hard angles reappeared on Mr. Stein's face. I glanced nervously at the chisel, but Mr. Stein kept talking. "It wasn't murder. *What could be*," he spat out. "That's what the blacksmith said, and that's all I wanted. Why shouldn't I have what other people take for granted? A happy home. A loving wife."

"Isabella found out, though, didn't she? She must've

suspected. Did she find the portrait? Is that why she took off the ring? And you started hating her."

Mr. Stein grinned, a gesture that concerned me slightly more than his scowl. "Yes, Bernie. You get it."

I shook my head. "No. No way."

"Come on, Bernie. You think I couldn't see how desperate you were for your father's attention the moment I walked into the den, and then all that longing over Isabella's portrait?" He shook his head in mock pity. "What about your mother? Is she giving you what you want? Poor little Bernie, trying so hard to be good and rubbing everyone the wrong way."

I couldn't have answered just then, even if I'd wanted to.

"You know what it's like to never get what you rightfully deserve. But the injustice, the inequalities in life, all even out in the end. Doesn't matter how heavy or light your heart is when you're dead. And, Bernie, I'll let you in on a little secret, balloon-like hearts are the easiest to puncture." Mr. Stein stopped here and stared hard at me. "All these lighthearted people around here: easy targets. I was doing you a favor, and you just couldn't leave it alone."

"You think I *wanted* all those people dead," I said, "just because they were happy?"

"No. Because they had what you didn't. Because they made others brighten in ways that you're not capable of." He glanced at Thomas's name on the family marker, and my heart sank with denial.

"Life around here needed more balance. If *we* can't have what we want, why should anyone else? *What could be*, right? Lives or stones, it feels good to crack them apart."

Mr. Stein turned his attention back to me. "Of course, once I heard from that dear Mimi of yours that you were headed off to Silverton . . . Cheerleading, was it?" Mr. Stein dipped his head and made a "tsk" sound with his tongue. "I knew you'd find out about the tools, even more than you'd already suspected, and that would be the end of our playful jousting. I knew you'd want the hammer and chisel for yourself, and we can't have that, can we?

"Luckily, I knew the best way to get rid of you . . . Seeing you yesterday was like seeing a ghost. You really shouldn't have been able to climb out of bed as close to finished as your portrait is."

The way I'd been feeling lately . . . I thought it was from all my fear and worry. Had it really been the portrait draining my strength down to that of a cracked and dry riverbed? As if to confirm it, Mr. Stein traced a line on my portrait, down the hollow of the neck, and I felt my throat closing off, the air being stolen from my lungs.

"And that thing with the soup — priceless. I'm really going to miss you, Bernie." Mr. Stein extended the hammer away from the chisel, into the night, and then back down. I felt the crack of iron against the stone as loudly as I heard it.

My entire body flinched this time, and then flooded with pain. My heart didn't feel strong, not in the slightest. But I *wanted* to live. And want was something my heart was used to. Even though I couldn't move, I could feel the want fighting inside me.

"Isabella's heart struggled right until the very end, as well. Resilience is built by hardship," Mr. Stein said. "That's why the cheery ones die so easily, and you're giving — me — so — much — trouble." Each word spoken was accented by a hammer swing and the chipping of granite. The tools began to glow red in his hands, looking as they must have all those years ago. Fresh from the blacksmith's smelting pot. Right before they were baked in bones.

Mr. Stein's white-laced eyes bore into me as he drew the hammer back one last time, and the ache in my heart pierced deeper. "Now let's put an end to all this nonsense, shall we?"

I thought of Mimi and Dad and even Michael. Then, I thought of my mama, my poor, heartbroken mama, about to lose a second child on this wicked day.

Mr. Stein's arm fell. Iron connected with iron, and stone cracked. The last thing I remembered before everything went black was the distant sound of a woman's voice crying out my name.

I CAME TO WITH COLD, CRISP GRASS BLADES CUTTING INTO my cheek. I was still alive. But how? My eyes and mouth gaped open as I gulped in the night air and at the same time I noticed the hammer and chisel on a patch of earth right in front of me. Not the shiny new ones — rather, the blacksmith's tools that spun this nightmare into being. They were still giving off a soft red glow, and I hopped up to snatch them — quick as a thief.

Mr. Stein was standing in the same place, next to my portrait. He was clear-eyed now, and for some reason he was cowering away, like he was afraid.

"Impossible," he said. "You're dead."

The tools felt icy-hot in my hands, and I felt a sudden surge of energy, just as I had the day I destroyed the portraits — only it was frightfully greater. Whatever power the tools possessed, I was now a part of it. I lunged forward. What I wanted shocked some deep-down part of me; but at the moment, I just didn't care. I wanted so badly I couldn't see straight, or right or left for that matter — just color. Everything radiated color — especially Mr. Stein. His heart beat bloodred.

Every pumping artery sent rays of crimson into the night.

And every pulse drew me closer. I took another step. I pointed the chisel at his heart. Mr. Stein clutched at his chest. The tools felt warmer and warmer in my hands as the beats of his heart began to slow.

Mr. Stein stumbled backward, wheezing and gasping for air, and his legs flew out in front of him. A loud CRACK rang through the cemetery as he knocked his head hard on the base of our family's monument. Then his body went still on the ground beneath me.

I stood over him, knowing even without a portrait, the tools could help me end his life. I wanted it. I wanted Mr. Stein's heart to stop — for Mrs. Finley and Mr. Fuller, even more for Isabella and Mrs. Evans. I wanted to feel the chisel break his skin and dig between his ribs, find the source of the pulsing red light and put it out. Forever.

"Bernie?" The sound of my name was closer this time, but still small, and shrill.

I stopped moving. The voice tugged at my heart, but the want was stronger. I bent down and pressed the chisel to the left side of Mr. Stein's chest. I raised the hammer.

"*Stop!*" The voice was louder now. I tried so hard to ignore it. To ignore her. But the voice was velvet smooth and chocolate sweet. "Please," she pleaded. "Bernie, please."

I turned my head and gasped, "Isabella?" A woman stood a few yards away. Her hair flowed in waves of soft yellow light. She wore a brilliant white gown and her own heart beat softer rays of red. When she parted her lips, the sound of my name came out on wings of blue and lilac — colors even more appealing than the bright red of Mr. Stein's heart.

I took a step away from Mr. Stein, and then another. I walked forward, wanting only to touch Isabella's ghost before her shimmering image vanished before my eyes yet again.

The tools yanked and pulled, trying to drive me back. But more than anything, I wanted to dip my fingers in the lavender lights streaking from Isabella's hands. I uncurled my fingers and let the tools slip.

Then all the colors wilted away. The power I'd felt was gone.

Only the image remained. It did not dissolve into the night and abandon me as it had after every nightmare. This image was earthly and real.

"Mama?" I whispered in confusion.

My mother was colorless in the night, her face ever as pale as the moon. Her hair, having grown in the months she'd locked herself away, now kissed the tips of her shoulder blades. Still dressed in her long white nightgown, her feet were pink, soft, and bare.

Mama reached her hands out to mine again, and I knew. Of course. The beating heart. It could never have been Isabella at all. Isabella's heart stopped weeks ago. My mama's, broken as it was, was still ticking.

I knew then that Mr. Stein had mistaken my mama for Isabella, just like I had. The thought of Isabella rising from the grave to seek her revenge must've frightened him into dropping the tools. However, the mistaken identity had caused me to let go of the hammer and chisel for an entirely different reason.

"Mama," I said again, this time rushing into her arms.

"Bernie, what's going on?" she said. I saw the way her eyes flicked from my portrait on the family monument to Mr. Stein lying unconscious on the ground beneath it. "Were you trying to kill that man, Bernie?" She shook her head like it couldn't be true. I was thankful for that. It meant even if she didn't think me saintly, she couldn't figure me for a murderer.

I wanted to tell her everything, replay every day from the moment Mr. Stein showed up, but just as I opened my mouth to speak, a bright light blinded me.

"Bernie!" Michael shouted. "Mrs. Morrison? Are you okay?" The beam from Michael's flashlight skipped from me to the marker and then played hopscotch over my portrait and along the body lying on the grass. "Holy cannoli, what happened?"

Before I could say anything, a second light appeared, crossing Michael's and lighting up the cemetery like a grand opening event. Sheriff Romano was breathing hard and looked a bit jumpy with one hand on her holster, and the other spotlighting the graveyard.

"Okay, Michael," she said, catching her breath. "This had better be important and not some sort of game." Just then, she seemed to notice Mr. Stein. He was starting to sit up, although rather woozily. Michael's mom dropped the flashlight so that light cut through the grass and bounced off the shiny replacement tools at Mr. Stein's feet. Sheriff Romano glanced at them, and then at my portrait, before swiftly yanking Mr. Stein's wrists behind his back and locking them in silver cuffs.

Michael and I exchanged a look as his mother pulled a pair of gloves from a pack near her holster and stretched them over her slender fingers. As she lifted the new tools from the dewy grass, Michael and I watched each other's faces. We were playing chicken. Who would say something first? Would either of us say anything at all?

It would've been the perfect time to come clean and to draw Sheriff Romano's attention to the second set of tools nearer my own feet. If the cursed hammer and chisel found their way into an endless vault of crime-scene evidence, it might keep them nearly as tucked away as if they were buried in a grave. However, my mind was still flooding with possibilities. Instead of directing Mrs. Romano to the proper tools, I scooted over an inch or two, closer to my mama, to where I could block the rusty hammer and chisel from Sheriff Romano's view.

Michael's eyebrows drew together and his dark eyes sunk deeper into his huge head. Did he know what I was up to? Did he disapprove?

I held my breath as his mother dropped the tools in a plastic bag, but Michael kept my secret from plunging from his lips.

"I'm still not sure what is going on here," Sheriff Romano said, measuring her words as she pulled Mr. Stein to his feet.

"But I suppose whatever it is warrants at least an explanation and possibly a stint in jail."

Mr. Stein turned his head sharply, away from Michael's mother.

"Looks like defamation of personal property to me, and . . ." Here Sheriff Romano glanced quickly at Michael and then back to Mr. Stein. "It sounds like I'll need some answers regarding a burglary and a fire in Silverton, as well."

Mrs. Romano turned back to Michael with a face that was both sternly hard and full of love. "What were you thinking?" she said. "You two are way too young to be playing detectives." She flashed her light at the portrait on my headstone, clucked her tongue, and then directed her gaze at me. "But I guess we're just lucky. This could've all ended a whole lot worse."

Michael and I both looked at our feet. Then, as Sheriff Romano began reading Mr. Stein his rights, Michael shifted his gaze to Mama, who was standing behind me and wavering like a strand of seaweed in an ocean's undercurrent. "What's she doing here?" he whispered.

"What's *your* mom doing here, and aren't you supposed to be hiding in the open space reserve?" I whispered back.

"Never made it there. As soon as I realized he wasn't after me, I ran straight to get Mom. And it's a good thing I did," Michael said defensively. "Mr. Stein obviously didn't stay knocked out for long. What would you have done if he came to before we arrived? How'd he get that way, anyhow?"

I eyed Mr. Stein, standing, waiting with his hands cuffed behind him. He seemed shorter by a few inches, or maybe his hair was just flatter. He also looked shaken and pitiful, and his eyes were dull and gray.

I shrugged. In a way, I kind of felt sorry for him.

"Michael, I need to get Mr. Stein processed, so let's get moving," his mom said. "I'm sure I'll have questions for you and Bernie both later, but that can wait."

Mrs. Romano fully took in the sight of my mother dressed in her nightgown, pink toes curled like rose petals in the grass. She hesitated. "Mrs. Morrison, will you and Bernie be all right? I can send a cruiser for you when we get back to the station," she said.

My mother looked more frail and childlike than I'd ever seen her. I took her hand in mine and shook my head. "It's not far. We'll walk home."

Mrs. Romano nodded and then pushed Abbot Stein in front of her. Michael slowly turned to follow her lead. "You're gonna tell me everything later, right?" he whispered.

"Everything," I said, hit with the realization that he'd probably be the only one I could tell.

After they were gone, I turned back to Mama. I was afraid she might be angry with me or disgusted by what she'd seen. I could only imagine how I'd looked to her — eyes glazed over and thirsty for Mr. Stein's blood.

"Let's sit for a while," I said, and pointed to the concrete bench.

Even as shocked and weary as she must've been, my mama was every bit as beautiful as Isabella. I felt a pang of jealousy knowing she hadn't come for me. It was my brother that had brought her here. Tonight was the anniversary of Thomas's death, and I was sure she'd come to visit his grave.

I dropped my head in shame and disappointment, but she lifted my chin with her bony fingers. "Bernie," she said. "Tell me what happened." Her cheeks reddened in the cool night breeze, and she shivered in her thin nightgown.

I stared down at her feet. My own heels were scaly and dry, the skin around my toenails cracked from a summer of wearing flip-flops all over town. The skin on my mama's feet was nearly translucent and perfectly smooth. They were the feet of someone who walked on clouds, or not at all, except for the dirt and grass that had soiled them tonight.

She shouldn't have to know what the night had nearly cost me. Cost us both. I couldn't protect her from the hardships she'd already faced, but I could protect her from that.

So I told her Mr. Stein was a bad man. He was a thief and an arsonist and a low-down, no-good creep. And Michael and I had tried to stop him — tried to steal the tools from him so we'd have proof of his wrongdoings. Really, it wasn't all a lie, just a shortened, watered-down version of the truth. It was the same story I'd tell Sheriff Romano later.

My mama and I huddled in silence after I finished weaving together the parts I felt like sharing. Then, like it was no more significant than an afterthought, I added, "Mr.

Stein must've etched my portrait up there just to frighten me off."

Mama looked at my portrait and narrowed her eyes at it. I was quite certain she wasn't buying it. I hadn't exactly explained why after stealing Mr. Stein's tools, I'd felt the need to bring them to the cemetery. I hadn't explained why I'd stood over Mr. Stein with the tools in my hands and why my eyes had clouded over (she had to have seen that, hadn't she?). I hadn't explained why I'd trailed behind her to the bench, first pausing to lift something from the grass, nor the clink she must've heard, followed by a second. I hadn't explained the toolbox cradled in my lap.

And my mama was no dummy.

But tonight, she didn't have the strength to question me. The strength necessary to doubt the story I'd gently fed her. Not when the headstone she came to see had been defiled with my portrait. And not with the heaviness of the memories she was already bearing.

I could see in her eyes that someday she'd ask me again about this night . . . and, hopefully, then I could tell her the truth. Hopefully, then she'd be able to hear it.

Mr. Stein had said my heart was hardier than most — my wanting, hurting heart, had brought me here. It had kept me going, even with my portrait so close to completion. So I had hope that Mama's heart, for all its pain and suffering, would heal someday, too. And be stronger for it.

"Do you want some time alone now, with . . . Thomas?" It was hard, so hard, to speak his name to my mama. I'd spent the past year pretending I'd forgotten it, forgotten him, every time I was around her. For her, or for me, I didn't know. But with all the truth I'd been running away from, I had to at least acknowledge why my mother was here.

Again, my mama tilted my chin with her thin fingers so that I had nowhere to look but the icy oceans of her eyes. "Thomas," she said, and then stopped herself. I had to wonder when she'd last spoken his name out loud. "Thomas . . . isn't here, nor is your grandfather. Those are their graves. That is all. I didn't come here tonight for either of them. If I had, I would've at least had the decency to get dressed first." My mama smiled softly — a REAL smile — and a butterfly flitted in the corner of my heart.

"After you shut the window tonight, I couldn't breathe. The air was too heavy and thick, and I was sticking to the sheets with sweat . . . and tears. I had to open it again. When I did, I saw you. And what you did with the soup. The boy and that wretched man ran off, and then by the time I found my voice to call your name through the window, you'd disappeared, as well. Mimi and your father were gone. I had no choice but to follow you."

My mama had come for me? The butterfly in my heart grew to the size of a meadowlark. "Thank you," I said, and I threw myself into her arms.

She swayed a little on the bench and then recovered, holding me tight. She was stronger than I thought. "Let's go home, Bernie."

We stood from the cold cement bench, still wrapped in each other's arms. "Soon, Mama," I said, pulling away from her. "Wait here for me. I won't be long. Promise."

What could be. What could be. All the way to Mrs. Evans's grave the words repeated in my head like the Gregorian chant Father John sometimes said at mass. I easily climbed under the ropes sectioning off the grave site, all hollowed out for Friday's ceremony. I stood with my toes at the edge of that deep, dark hole. *What could be. What could be.*

As if they knew I was still wavering, and in an attempt to sway my decision, the lock box heated in my hands. Warm like a loaf of bread straight from the oven. Hard to let go of.

There were so many possibilities. The word *anything* floated into my brain as if answering the chant. *What could be? What could be? Anything.*

But how well had "anything" worked out for Mr. Stein, for Isabella, or even Isabella's father? (I got the impression he wasn't all that well liked in Silverton.) Perhaps "anything" brought along its own special flavor of heartache.

And then, my mama's voice rang through the cemetery yet again. "Bernie!"

Her voice — her love, rather — had drawn me from the tools once before, and it reminded me again of all that I had: a mama who'd finally left her room for the sole purpose of finding me in a darkened graveyard, a grandmother who (mad as she'd be when she learned of all this) would undoubtedly continue to rise early in the morning and fix me breakfast, a father who had rushed to my side when I felt weak and afraid . . . and a friend. A friend who I had pushed away, again and again, and who still came back and knowingly risked his life for me. For the first time in a very long while, my heart didn't feel all that wanting.

The box cooled in my hands as I let it slide. "I'm coming, Mama," I answered.

Mama was standing beside the family headstone when I returned. "I just have one question, Bernie," she said.

Uh-oh, I thought. *Here we go.*

"Where did the woman go?"

Of all the questions she could've asked, this was the last one I would've expected. "What woman? Sheriff Romano?" I asked.

"No. When I left the house, I couldn't see you anywhere. But there was this woman. At first I was afraid. I thought she might be with that horrible Mr. Stein, but then she was beckoning me to follow, and I didn't know what else to do. I followed her here to the cemetery. Then, once we were inside . . . It was like she vanished," my mama said, and then added, "She was almost too beautiful to be real."

CHAPTER NINETEEN

ISABELLA DID NOT VISIT THAT NIGHT. EVEN THOUGH I SLEPT
with her portrait tucked under my pillow like a little girl waiting on the Tooth Fairy, the foot of my bed remained vacant.
My dreams, hollow. I wanted to know if she was pleased, if she
would've done the same with the tools, given the option.
Perhaps her silence was the answer. Perhaps she was finally at
peace.

At Mrs. Evans's burial the next day, Mama stood locked
between Mimi and me. Dad stood as hard and unmoving as
one of his monuments behind her. I held my breath as the casket was lowered into the ground. I didn't hear a single word
Father John said. I just imagined the tools glowing red with
fury as the earth tumbled down on the box that jailed them
there. Michael, who was standing on the other side of Mrs.
Evans's grave with both of his parents, caught my eye and gave
me a small but encouraging smile.

Mimi had put up a fuss right before we came. She said it
wouldn't do Mama an ounce of good to watch dirt being shov-
eled over yet another coffin lid. But Mama had insisted on
coming. Just like I'd insisted that Mama join us in the kitchen
for breakfast.

Mama and I had both been in bed by the time he and Mimi had returned from the rosary service. So when Sheriff Romano called first thing in the morning to check on us and wound up filling Dad in on everything, my father let loose a mighty long string of nursery rhymes. As proof that they knew nothing of the previous night's events, Mimi had been fixing up two trays when the phone rang.

Just as Dad was saying "Old Mother Hubbard" into the receiver, I slipped quickly and quietly back up the stairs. I crept into Mama's room and went directly to the woolen curtains. I ripped them open, assaulting the room with light. My mama darted up in bed, shielding her eyes from the sunlight. "Bernie? What's going on?"

Mr. Stein had been right about one thing: He and I both knew what it was like to have our hearts broken, to want something we couldn't have. But what made me different, and the very reason I was able to let go of the iron hammer and chisel when he couldn't, was that I knew there were people who loved me.

I'm not saying things are perfect now. And how I ever thought learning to etch portraits was the answer to fixing it all is beyond me. I'm also not saying that the want has forever drained itself from my heart, but that's not necessarily a bad thing. Want made me stronger. It made me go after what was really important — which is all you can do when things are broken.

You can't wait on someone else to put the pieces back

together. Even if you're afraid, or you don't feel like the right person for the job, you still have to do what you can to remind the people in your life that they are loved and needed, too. Otherwise, God forbid, all those cracks might scab over in ugly and twisted ways — like the cracks in Mr. Stein's heart had — instead of healing.

I wasn't about to let that happen to my mama. "C'mon," I said. "Get up. You came when I needed you last night, and I need you even more now." I laced her fingers in mine and pulled her to her feet. She wore the same white gown she'd worn to the cemetery, and her cheeks had kept some of their pinkness from the night before.

Mama seemed to drift like a buoy in my wake as she floated down the stairs, and I scrambled in front of her. My face appeared in the kitchen first and was met with angry and condemning glares. The phone was back on the wall and Mimi and Dad looked all revved up to give me what for. Then they saw Mama trailing behind me, and the moment was sweetened and snapped in half like a sugar pea.

Mama drew in close beside me. "Mmmm," she said. "Smells like cinnamon. What's for breakfast?"

After all that had happened, I didn't know what to do with Isabella's portrait, but then I learned that she had an unmarked grave. With no known heirs, arrangements for a headstone had not been made. Luckily, Dad agreed to inset Isabella's portrait into one of the blank monuments from our backyard, and two

Sundays later, he drove Michael and me and the headstone to the Silverton Cemetery.

As we placed the marker at the head of Isabella Freemont's grave, Michael said, "The flower turned out nice."

"Thanks." I smiled. Not only had Dad agreed to donate one of our blanks, he'd also used one of my sketches to sand-blast a lily into the stone next to Isabella's portrait. Dad smiled at Michael's comment, too, and once the monument was lev-eled above the grave, he started to wander off in his quiet way.

"Wait, Dad!" I said, and I wrapped my arms around his belly. "Thanks." He patted my hair with his hand before returning to the truck to wait on us.

Michael stood by my side staring at the portrait. "Don't you think it's a little creepy using Mr. Stein's handiwork as part of the headstone?"

"Oh, I don't know," I said. "I think the portrait belongs to Isabella now. She's been right beside me these past few weeks and, well, even though I can't really explain it, I think the por-trait's why."

Michael seemed to accept that. He nodded and then said, "My uncle was able to match Mr. Stein's fingerprints to ones left on a can of fuel found near the fire. The case is pretty much in the bag."

The story Michael had fed his mother had been similar enough to the one I'd told Mama in the cemetery that nobody thought to question the darker, underlying evil and the myste-rious deaths that had occurred. Even if we had gone and told everyone the whole truth, what Mr. Stein was really guilty of, it could never be proven in a court of law.

"Good," I said, although it didn't seem like enough. Mr. Stein caused all those deaths, and he would just go to jail for arson. How many years until he got out? Five or six? Maybe a little longer since I couldn't imagine any jury or judge taking a liking to him. I felt my body quake slightly, and Michael slung his arm over my shoulder.

"You're not thinking about trying to kiss me again, are you?" I asked.

Michael grinned. "Maybe."

"Ugh. What is it with you and cemeteries?"

"What is it with *you* and cemeteries?"

"Fine. Let's go. We need to get back to Stratwood anyway. We have somewhere to be, right?" It was easy to convince Michael to join the outreach committee. The one Sacred Heart was putting together — even without Mrs. Evans to head it. He was, of course, looking for something else to keep him busy. And me? I'm gonna do all I can to keep the lonely, broken hearts of Stratwood from turning bitter and disfigured. I know all too well what can happen if they do.

I slipped my fingers between Michael's much wider ones, and we began walking away from Isabella's grave. (Hopefully the last one we'll be visiting for a very long time.) As we did, I lifted up on my tiptoes just high enough to kiss Michael Romano squarely on the cheek. Then, walking hand in hand, we left the graveyard together.

THE
END

ACKNOWLEDGMENTS

From story spark to book, so many people have helped me chisel out the words appearing on these pages or have lifted my spirits along the way.

Michael Stearns, thank you for believing in this story long before there was any reason to. Your early enthusiasm carried me through.

Anna Webman, thank you for aptly guiding me through numerous revisions, for listening to me ramble endlessly on the phone, and for somehow, through it all, helping me to un-muddle things.

Ginger Knowlton, thank you for keeping me at Curtis Brown and for treating me keenly. I feel very secure with you at the helm.

To all the dedicated souls at Scholastic — I am forever grateful. A special thanks to Rachel Griffiths, who opened the door, and to my delightfully eloquent and brilliant editor, Mallory Kass, who made it feel like home.

Dad, thank you for (perhaps unintentionally) teaching me the art of storytelling.

Mom — ever my first reader — thank you for gushing over everything I've ever written (even the stuff that was not so good).

My in-laws, especially Jane Goebel, thank you for sharing in and supporting my reading addiction.

Courtney Waters, what a tremendous show of friendship it was when you dropped all things consuming to give me valuable feedback in an insanely short amount of time. No amount of pumpkin bread could ever be sufficient in repaying you.

Jennifer Soderfelt, my dear, lifelong friend, you and your students will continue to be my test subjects, won't you? Thanks.

To James and Kristen Davenport and other close family and friends, thank you for being the wonderful people that you are. You've all supported me, and thereby this book, in ways immeasurable.

Ethan, Logan, and Lucas, thank you for understanding all the times Mommy needed a few extra minutes at the computer, and to my husband, Matt, for quietly shutting the door to the office when those minutes extended into hours.

And my greatest thanks to God, who knows and guides my heart.